Olympia Heights:
The Blood of Athens

By Amy Leigh Strickland

*To all of the English teachers who inspired
me to write and taught me to love reading.*

"You should reach the limits of virtue, before you cross the border of death."

-Tyrtaeus

The Pantheon

Zach Jacobs (Zeus)

June Herald (Hera)

Nick Morrisey (Poseidon)

Valerie Hess (Hestia)

Dr. Celene Davis (Demeter)

Frank Guerrero (Ares)

Peter Hadley (Hades)

Devon Valentine (Aphrodite)

Miranda "Minnie" Rutherford (Athena)

Evan Fuller (Hephaestus)

Teddy Wexler Jr. (Dionysus)

Penelope Davis (Persephone)

Astin Hill (Apollo)

Diana Hill (Artemis)

Lewis Mercer (Hermes)

Dr. Jason Livingstone (Mortal)

OLYMPIA HEIGHTS

Book 3
The Blood of Athens

by Amy Leigh Strickland

"To give birth is a fearsome thing; there is no hating the child one has borne even when injured by it."

-Sophocles

i.

Because Alkmene carried a son of Zeus,
she invited the full force of Hera's wrath,
who sent Eileithyia, goddess of childbirth,
to stay her labor.

Eileithyia delayed the birth of the child
until the wait endangered mother and son,
but a handmaid with no fealty to Hera
took pity on them.

As a trick, to startle the watchful goddess,
the handmaid suddenly yelled, "A son is born!"
Eileithyia was confused by this statement
and let slip her guard.

That moment of chaos was all they needed
for the head to crown and a face to appear.
With a sharp cry, Hera's vengeance was thwarted.
Herakles was born.

"A society grows great when old men plant trees whose shade they know they shall never sit in."

-Greek Proverb

I.

Mr. Hadley sat on the end of his bed, dabbing a wet facecloth against his knuckles. He had lost his temper again. He was sorry to say that most of the blood on his hand was not his own.

He stretched his fingers, feeling the split skin strain and scream with pain. He had never wanted the boy; she knew that, but he had agreed for her sake. His wife had wanted Peter so badly, and when she had bled to death bringing him into the world, Mr. Hadley had lost everything.

He heard a sound outside of his bedroom. It was a footstep on old, cracked, pistachio linoleum. He was about to fly into another rage. How dare that boy sneak out after everything that had just happened! The bedroom doorknob turned and opened. Mr. Hadley waited, but no one was there.

"What the--?" He approached the door to close it, but he was interrupted by another sound. He spun around. The VCR on his old tube television was accepting a tape.

The play button depressed as if it were being pushed by an invisible hand. The television flicked on.

Mr. Hadley stood frozen in amazement as a video played. It began with a scene in his kitchen three weeks before. It seemed to be filmed from between a stack of soup cans, their blurred silhouettes looming in the foreground of the low-quality video. Peter knocked a glass off the counter. He did it on purpose? Mr. Hadley watched himself tear into the room, shouting. Peter said something back, and Mr. Hadley flat-out punched him in the jaw. The boy's head whipped around and barely missed the counter before dropping out of frame. Mr. Hadley kept shouting, his wild, bearded face red with anger and spit flying from his mouth.

The video stopped and was replaced by Peter's bruised face. He was sitting in a janitorial closet, probably at school, and he was holding the camera. His black eyes were fixed on the lens, staring through the camera and the television to lock eyes with his father.

"Dad," he said, his voice trembling even to say it in a recording. "I have three weeks of this stuff on tape. I've given it to friends-- and no, not Penny, so don't even think about trying to intimidate her. A grown up has a copy. So you have a decision to make."

Peter took a deep breath. His voice became steady and he stopped trembling. "You can either lay off the booze and keep your hands to yourself, or I'll have you put away for a long time. Anything happens to me and people know what to do. I'm seventeen, I can get a court order to live on my own for six more months while you rot in prison."

"Dad," he said, bringing the camera closer to his face. The autofocus couldn't adjust, leaving his features blurred. "Keep your damned hands off of me or I will take you down. Sleep tight."

The door to the bedroom closed. Mr. Hadley sat on the bed. It was his turn to quake with fear.

He stood up and crossed the room. The bedroom doorknob was made of cheap metal and painted over gold. The paint had chipped away over the years to reveal its true nature. Mr. Hadley locked it and shook the door to be sure that it was tight.

The threats of the tape were not what held him in terror. It was Peter. Mr. Hadley had witnessed him a handful of times over the past year talking to absolutely nobody. That boy had never been right. How had he come in here and played that tape without being seen?

"I'm her Doctor," Jason Livingstone said, trying to keep his voice level as he spoke to the receptionist at Mercy Hospital. "Dr. Jason Livingstone."

The large woman slipped her thick, black glasses down her nose and looked closely at Devon's file. "Livingstone?" She raised an eyebrow and smirked.

"Yes," he said. "Livingstone." He glanced towards the elevator door. This was it. This was the moment when they found out if the baby was going to give them all away.

"Oh, yes. Here you are. She's in room 319."

Jason ran down the hall. The receptionist called after him. He tapped his foot as the elevator brought him to the third floor. A nurse, who must have been alerted, cut him off before he reached the door.

"Sir, this room is sterile. If you follow me, I can get you prepped."

Devon screamed from the other side of the door.

"Is she already delivering?" he asked.

"She's already at nine centimeters."

Jason wasn't going to waste time arguing with the nurse. He followed her to a sink and washed up while she brought him a gown, mask, and gloves. Five minutes later, he entered the delivery room. Devon was laid back on the bed, her feet propped up in stirrups. Sweat covered her forehead. Frank stood next to her, holding her tiny hand in his own massive one. He looked scared.

"Doc," he said, when Jason entered.

"How's she doing?"

Devon screamed. She dug her nails into Frank's hand. He didn't flinch. The contractions were coming close together now.

"Alright, Devon," said the doctor at her feet. She was a middle-aged hispanic woman with streaks of grey in her black hair. "I'm going to need you to push. He's almost here."

Jason had been in a delivery room many times before. He had observed a few times in med school, assisted when they were short staffed at the hospital, and he had witnessed the birth of his own three children. Watching Devon now, he was amazed at how glamorous she managed to look, screaming, red-faced, with her blonde hair drenched in sweat.

"One more push," the doctor said.

The last push came with a screamed expletive and then Devon collapsed back on the bed, panting. Jason rushed to get a look at the infant as he was brought to the sink to be cleaned up.

Ten fingers. Ten toes. No horns. No hooves. He sighed and turned to Frank, giving the thumbs up. Frank's smile melted his hardened exterior. For a moment, the colossal eighteen-year-old looked like a child.

Frank pressed his forehead to the glass, looking in on the nursery and the row of baby boys and girls lined up orderly and classified by pink and blue. Jason approached and stopped at his side, watching the massive young man for a sign of what he was thinking.

"Do you know which one's yours?" he asked Frank, tapping his arm and handing him a cup of coffee. Frank took the cup and nodded thanks. It was one in the morning now. He was running on adrenaline.

"Third row away from us, six in from the left," he said. "That's him. I can tell."

Jason squinted through the glass at the infant. The baby boy was very pink, and his hair was hidden in a blue hospital cap.

"What's his name?" Jason asked.

"Minnie found something for us," Frank replied. "Xander. It's Greek. It means defender of the people."

"Does Xander have a middle name?"

"Devon." Jason smiled. Frank did, too. "She's a little vain," he said. Jason laughed.

"Every heart sings a song, incomplete, until another heart whispers back. Those who wish to sing always find a song. At the touch of a lover, everyone becomes a poet."

-Plato

ii.

It was the night of Harmonia's wedding
when the goddess of fertility first laid
eyes on the beautiful hero, Iason,
and knew she loved him.

They met in a field she had blessed with bounty.
The field had been plowed three times and left fallow
so that she could restore its fertility.
They met in darkness.

The hero of the harvest took her in arms
and the two made love in the naked wheat field.
Then they, gathering their clothes about themselves,
returned to the feast.

"Sex and sleep alone make me conscious that I am mortal."

  -Alexander The Great

II.

Jason set the alarm on his phone and climbed into the back seat of his Buick Electra for a nap. He had an hour before he needed to go get Celene, and he didn't want to stop at home and wake the kids or the sitter. Being at the hospital all night reminded him of his late twenties, when he had pulled double night shifts once a week and slept other evenings in the on-call room. He had been younger then, and his body was better equipped for sleep deprivation. Being reminded of those times did not make him feel younger tonight. It reminded him that he was only getting older.

When his phone buzzed fifty minutes later, Jason shot up and smacked his head on the upholstered roof of the car. He climbed into the front seat and made his first stop at the Dunkin' Donuts drive through. At exactly five thirty in the morning, he pulled up at Celene Davis' house, caffeinated and thoroughly disheveled.

Jason knocked on the door.

Penny Davis answered it. She was fifteen, a sophomore in high school, and the youngest member of The Pantheon. Her heart-shaped face, lately marked with thick black eyeliner and pink glitter lipstick, was clean of all makeup. It was just too early for any of that nonesense. Jason had been dating Penny's mother for nearly seven months, and Penny had become quite comfortable with Jason.

"You look like crap," she said, sparing him no politeness.

"Devon had the baby a few hours ago," he explained.

"She did?"

"Normal. No horns."

Penny laughed. "Awesome. Come on in. Mom's not really super-cheery this morning, either." Penny turned into the small house and hollered back towards the bedroom. "Mom, Jason's here. Devon had the baby. It's normal!"

Jason came inside and shut the door. It was a cool March morning, which was downright frigid by Miami standards.

"Penny, I can't make out a word you're saying," Celene shouted from the bathroom.

"I said, Devon had the baby!"

Celene Davis came out of the bathroom, zipping a plastic bag of travel shampoo bottles and walking towards her packed suitcase. She had not foregone makeup this morning. Her green eyes, framed with thick lashes, were surrounded by a subtle shading of brown eye shadow. She wore a coffee colored lipstick that made all of her features pop. Jason had not stopped being impressed by her cat-like beauty. "Oh, Jason."

Jason crossed the room to kiss Celene. Penny tactfully looked away.

"No offense, you look like hell."

"I was watching Devon deliver a baby all night," he said.

"Is it--?"

"Normal." Jason nodded. "Xander Devon Guerrero. Totally, absolutely healthy and normal."

"Thank God," Celene said. "Are you sure you're good to drive?"

"I've had coffee. You forget I used to pull doubles at the emergency room."

"You were much younger," she said.

Jason grunted.

Celene tucked the plastic bag of toiletries in her purse and Jason picked up her suitcase. Penny dragged her own (bright pink) behind her on wheels. "Off we go, then," Jason said. "You'll need plenty of time to get through security."

A mob of sleepy teenagers stood, clustered next to airport security. Screens all over the terminal showed boarding times, safety announcements, and muted CNN reports about a European serial killer. The international airport was sparsely decorated with white concrete columns, white tile, potted palms, and posters for local tourist destinations.

It was a massive space with ceilings three-stories high. A powered cart towed a train of luggage carts past check-in as they entered through the giant revolving door. The occasional state-funded art installation filled dead space at the corners of the terminal.

Penny ran ahead of her mother and vanished among the sea of hoodies and backpacks. A few of the faculty members were already scanning the crowd and checking off names on a roster.

Candice Matthews, a frizzy, red-haired English teacher, shot a glare at Celene as she turned to say goodbye to Jason. Candice had held a torch for Jason for quite some.

Jason took Celene's hand and pulled her around behind a concrete column. "I know you're there to chaperone, but remember to have fun. It's not every day you get a free trip to Athens."

Celene smiled and stretched on her toes to kiss him. She wasn't wearing her usual high heels to fly. "Promise you'll miss me?"

"I already do," Jason smiled.

"It's only a week." She slid her arms around his back and rested her head on his chest. Nothing brought two people together quite like ancient secrets and mortal peril. When she finally lifted her head, she stayed close and whispered. "I'll be back in time to celebrate your birthday."

"I haven't looked forward to one of those in almost ten years."

"You should get a sitter for this one," Celene said.

"We can go out," Jason started to suggest.

"I was thinking they could go out and we could stay in."

"Oh." He hesitated and then raised an eyebrow, "Oh?"

"Oh," she said with a smile and stepped away. Jason had been a perfect gentleman for the last seven months, but he liked the sound of this plan. "Well, I'm definitely looking forward to this birthday."

Celene grabbed the handle of her suitcase and pulled it up. "I suppose I need to check in with Candice. It's time to go get groped by airport security."

Jason slid his hands into his pockets. "Stay safe over there," he said. "Keep your eyes on our bunch."

"There aren't enough eyes in the world for that job," she joked.

Jason kissed Celene one last time and then watched her walk towards the crowd of students.

Peter Hadley, a tall, pale boy with dark hair, turned to look at Jason. Jason waved. Peter broke away from the crowd.

"How's it going?" Jason asked him, keeping his voice low.

"Alright. I mean... yeah. Free trip to Greece for being the poorest kid in school. Can't knock that."

Jason cast a skeptical eye over the boy. He had no visible bruises, but that didn't mean that everything was okay. This fall, Peter had come to Jason with a secret. Jason already knew that Peter was Hades, Lord of the Dead, able to speak to ghosts and turn invisible. What was one more secret? As far as Jason knew, only he, Celene, and Penny knew this secret. Peter had been suffering in an abusive home for most of his life and Penny had talked him into getting help.

Jason was trying to help, but the normal procedure of reporting to DHR wouldn't work here. Peter didn't want to leave Olympia Heights in case another Titan popped up. He also didn't want to end up in a foster home in case his cover was blown. That left few options. Peter had caught a beating on tape and was blackmailing his father with it. Jason knew that this solution wasn't going to last and had been working on an alternate plan.

"Listen," Jason said, "When you get back, come to my office. I have a friend you need to meet."

"A friend? You mean a lawyer?"

"He specializes in emancipation of minors," Jason explained in a hushed tone.

"I've got it under control," Peter said.

Jason shook his head. "The tape is a stopgap. We can get you a room at the Youth Initiative, you pay expenses with your wages from work, and everyone in The Pantheon helps out a little."

"I dunno."

"Think about it. You have a whole week in Greece to decide."

"He's afraid of me now," Peter said. "He hasn't laid a hand on me in two weeks."

"Peter," Jason shook his head.

Peter didn't let him finish his thought. "I gotta go. We're moving."

Indeed, the crowd of students from Olympia Heights had started to move towards the security lane. Peter darted back to where Penny stood, guarding his black duffel bag.

Jason watched as Celene herded twenty-four teenagers towards the back of the line.

He checked his watch. Jamie and Scotty would be waking up soon. He waved one last time to Celene and headed for airport parking. Maybe, if he was lucky, he could plug in *My Neighbor Totoro* and get an hour nap before all hell broke loose.

"As to marriage or celibacy, let a man take which course he will, he will be sure to repent."

-Socrates

iii.

The bird sat on a branch outside her window,
carefully nursing its outstretched, wounded wing.
With a cream colored breast and grey crested head,
it was beautiful.

Hera spotted the damaged Cuckoo and brought
it into the small, seas-side hut where she lived.
Once inside, the little bird shifted and changed:
Zeus stood before her.

Impressed with his trick, the goddess let him stay
and before very long they fell into bed.
This is how mighty Zeus, the king of the gods
won himself a queen.

"When a match has equal partners then I fear not."

-Aeschylus

III.

Zach Jacobs heard the front door close. His mother was on her way to church. He looked over at the glowing red numbers on his alarm clock. The plane had already left. Two thirds of the football team and half of The Pantheon were on their way to Greece.

Zach climbed out of bed, gently turning back the black t-shirt sheets, careful not to disturb June, and crossed the hall to get a drink of water from the bathroom. The tiny bathroom had tile that ran half-way up the walls and then gave way to yellowed white paint. Zach turned the ceramic knobs on the sink and dipped his head under the tap, drinking chlorinated town water. When he came back into the room, June was awake, quietly watching him. A look of maturity had settled on her features over the last two years. She was growing into a woman. Her tight ponytail had come loose in the night and June tugged at the covered elastic, letting her fire red hair fall to her shoulders.

"Are you alright?" she asked, sitting up.

"I'm fine," he said. Zach sat down on the bed. "Thirsty."

"Fine? You're not still bummed that your Dad wouldn't pay for Greece, are you?"

"You could have gone, you know," he said. Zach set the water on his night stand. "I can last one week on my own."

June slipped her hand into his and nodded, "I know. But what fun would it be, seeing Greece without you?"

Zach raised an eyebrow. He still suspected that June had stayed home to keep an eye on him. He didn't exactly have a chaste past, but he had been faithful since their August reunion. "I dunno. It's Athens. I guess I just hoped that being there would spark some memories. We still don't have very many answers. We know what we are, but why?"

June let go of his hand and wrapped her arms around his shoulders, leaning on his back. Her red hair tickled the back of his neck. "That's a stretch, Zach. It might be where we come from, but Greece these days is no more spiritual or mysterious than America. Besides, who wants to go visit a country with a collapsing economy and spend the entire week with teachers breathing down their necks?"

"When you put it that way..."

"Seriously, Zach. Can you honestly say you'd rather be on that plane with Nick than sitting in your bed here, with me?"

Zach grinned. He turned around and wrapped his arms around his girlfriend. His stubble scratched her face as he kissed her. "This is better," he said, breaking the kiss so that his lips could venture down to her neck. "Sexy girlfriend, beautiful weather, no adult supervision."

June laughed as he nipped at her ear. She had learned to relax quite a bit over the past few months. The summer before had nearly resulted in a complete mental break down, but June had learned to recognize when she was being irrational or uptight.

Zach didn't care that his face felt like sandpaper or that June had morning breath. He could feel her breasts, free from the constraints of a bra, just below her tank top, pressed against his chest. Zach pressed his hips forward and let out a little moan. This was way better than Athens.

June's arms tensed. "Zach," she said, hesitating. She could tell that she had accidentally started something. "Zach, wait."

"June," he whined.

"Zach," she said, a little more severely.

Zach sat up. "Alright." He held his hands up in surrender as he rose to walk to the bathroom. June pulled the black cotton sheets up and crossed her arms over her chest. "Zach," she called.

It was quiet for a minute, and then Zach came back into the bedroom. He grabbed a pair of jeans off the floor and put them on.

"I'm sorry," June said.

"Don't be."

"Zach..." she left his name hanging in the air, the opening clause to a sentence she didn't know how to finish.

"It's fine. I mean... we've been together for how many years?"

"I don't want to count before, Zach. It wasn't good, then. You-- we weren't good to each other."

"And I cheated," he said. It was something he rarely admitted out loud. "A lot."

"And I manipulated you. We weren't good for each other. I'm not blaming you Zach."

"We've been together for for seven months, then."

June shook her head. She climbed out of bed and picked up the large, black, slouch bag that held a change of clothes. Her parents knew she was sleeping over a friend's house. They had assumed it was a *girl* friend. "It's not about time."

"We're eighteen," Zach added. "Eighteen. And you wouldn't be here if you were worried about your parents."

"It's not about being eighteen or being together for a predetermined amount of time, Zach," June snapped. She took a deep breath and started pulling clothing out of her bag. "Yes, for a while I thought it was about that, but it's not. I've had a lot of time to think and to know what I want. I do want to have sex with you, Zach, but I want you to be the first, the last, the only."

"And I've cheated." Zach crossed to June and wrapped his arms around her. She dropped the pair of jeans in her hand and relaxed against him.

"I don't want to wait until marriage because society or church or my mother tells me to. I know it's stupid with the fifty percent divorce rate, but I want to wait because I want to be sure that the first person I give myself to is the last. Is the only."

"That's not stupid." Zach had played the field enough this past summer to know that having sex with a lot of different beautiful women, while fun at first, was highly overrated. He held June for a while, letting the tension of the moment fall away.

"I love you," she finally whispered, "And I trust you. But--"

June didn't get to finish. Zach was on his knee.

"No!" she said. "Get up. You are not proposing to me so that I'll have sex with you."

Zach laughed, "I'm not."

"You're not proposing?"

"Oh, no. I am proposing. Will you stop talking long enough to let me do that?"

June opened and closed her mouth.

"Good." Zach took her hand. "Now, I don't know how old we are. Three thousand, four thousand, a million years old? We're already married. I may have seduced a couple of women disguised as an animal and you might have horribly massacred them, but we keep coming back to each other. I'd like to think that after all of these years, I've grown. You have, too. I had you for thousands of years and I couldn't stand six months apart. I love you, and even when we drive each other to do insane things, we always find each other again. So I'm not asking you, June Herald, the eighteen-year-old girl, to run away and marry Zach Jacobs, the horny teenager. I'm asking you, June, my Queen, goddess, to renew your vows to me."

There were tears in June's eyes. It was unprecedented.

"That's really sweet, Zach," she finally said. "Maybe next lifetime you shouldn't include massacre in a marriage proposal."

Zach squeezed her hand. A faint surge of energy passed from his fingertips and along with it, the echo of a memory. It was pure happiness, and she knew that it was associated with some lost memory of her wedding night with Zeus. They were made for each other.

"Alright," she said, nodding. A small smile turned up the corners of her lips. "I'll marry you."

Zach jumped up, grinning, and picked her up. June clung to him, afraid that he might drop her.

"Let's go today," he said, setting her back down on his bedroom floor.

June shook her head, "You have to wait like, a month, in Florida. You have to file for a license and then wait."

"But you don't in Georgia," Zach said.

June cocked her head. "You're serious?"

"Totally. You can tell your mom you've gone camping with some friends from school and I'll tell mine that I'm in Orlando with my dad. It's only a few hours drive. We can be there by sun down."

June chewed on her lip for a moment. She nodded, "Alright. Savannah, Georgia."

Zach pumped his fist and ran to his closet for a duffel bag.

June picked up her jeans off the floor and started towards the bathroom to change. She closed the bathroom door and sat down on the wooden lid of the toilet. She had always planned to graduate from a top college, marry Zach, get him into a political office, and become the first lady some day. Finding out that they were Greek Gods had temporarily derailed her ambitions. She smiled as she thought about this plan, one she had plotted every day for most of her life. It was back on track now. Who cared if it was a little out of order?

"The art of living well and the art of dying well are one."

-Epicurus

iv.

The spear of Achilles struck bold Telaphus
and tore a fatal wound in the soldier's thigh.
Telephaus knew that, without help, he was dead
and grew desperate.

With a terrible fear of losing his life,
Telaphus snatched up the young boy, Orestes.
He held the dagger to his throat and threatened
to end the boy's life.

The small boy was very dear to his mother.
Achilles was left with no other option.
He had to heal the villian, his enemy,
to save the young boy.

Achilles knew of a kind of old magic
that allowed the weapon to be the savior.
He scraped the bronze of his spear onto the wound:
Telaphus was healed.

"Knowledge becomes evil if the aim be not virtuous."

-Plato

IV.

Jason found himself at Tamiami Park that afternoon, watching Haley take turns pushing Scotty and Jamie on the big, red, bucket-seat swings at the playground. He sipped from his thermos of iced coffee and pushed his aviator sunglasses back up his nose. His skin was covered in a thin layer of perspiration and the glasses soon slid back down.

He had only gotten an hour and a half to nap before the credits were rolling on his *My Neighbor Totoro* DVD and the twins were trying to get into something messy. At least Haley was smart enough to wake her father before trouble started. She was a good girl.

Jason pulled out his phone and checked the application he had downloaded to track the flight. Celene and Penny were somewhere over the Atlantic Ocean. They wouldn't land until after dinner time here, which would be after three in the morning in Athens.

Someone sat down next to Jason. He looked up from his phone to make sure that his kids were still playing safely. He glanced casually at the man in his peripheral vision. The stranger wore sunglasses and a suede sports coat. He had dark, receding hair and ears that stuck out. The man cleared his throat. "I think it's a little toasty for this coat."

Jason nodded. "It's supposed to be eighty by mid-afternoon."

Jason took a long sip of his coffee and surveyed the playground, trying to guess which kids belonged to the stranger. Scotty was now trying to swing on his stomach and Jamie was copying his twin. Haley had found a big earthworm to poke at in the dirt.

Jason was just starting to consider calling Frank (to check in on Devon and the baby) when the stranger spoke again.

"They're all on their way to Greece, huh?"

Jason's back stiffened.

"It seems appropriate," he went on. "Thematic."

Jason could hear his pulse behind his eardrums. *Keep cool,* he thought. Jason tipped his phone so that the stranger couldn't see the screen in the sun and selected the option to record. "Who went to Greece?" he asked, playing dumb.

"Dr. Davis and her band of misfits. You know, your girlfriend."

Jason recalled June and Astin both reporting strange encounters last summer. A man at the cemetery had made a cryptic comment to Astin about the death of Diana's boyfriend, Ryan Bear. A similar-looking man had shown

June a passage from a book of mythology at a fair. It had curiously been about Hera. This man seemed to fit that description. "I'm not sure how you know Celene," Jason said, wondering if he should grab his kids and run, "But she is a teacher, so yes, she's chaperoning a field trip."

The stranger laughed. "Do I need to show you pictures?"

"Pictures?"

"I do have them, you know. Not here, of course, but we can make an appointment."

"Listen--" Jason started.

"No, you listen," the stranger said. Jason kept his eyes on his children, but he could see the man looming close in his peripheral vision. "I *know*. It was really my lucky break. I normally get paid to spy on cheating husbands. Imagine my surprise when I saw them all arrive to spend the night with Teddy junior. One was enough to seal your fate, but I did some digging, too. If you think I'm going to ignore three murders and a whole lot of unique abilities, you're even more naïve than I thought. "

"What do you want?"

The stranger stood up and pulled a handkerchief from his pocket. He blotted the sweat from his forehead. Jason turned to watch him, finally getting a real, good look at the stranger. The man put the pocket square away and drew a small metal case out of his pocket. He opened it and handed Jason a business card. "The moment they get back, we need to talk. It's going to take a lot to make me forget what I've seen."

Jason looked down at the business card. *Mr. Spade. Private Investigator.* Jason watched Spade walk back towards the parking lot. His fist balled around the business card. He knew things had been going a bit too smoothly; there was just no way to keep fifteen super-humans a secret when everyone had cameras on their phones. He cursed and shoved the card into his pocket.

"Haley, Jamie, Scotty!" he shouted. "Let's go." This park didn't feel safe any more.

"It is not enough to win a war; it is more important to organize the peace."

-Aristotle

V.

When the war between the Gods and the Titans
had ended, and the Olympians had won,
it came time for the three brothers to draw lots
to choose a domain.

Zeus, the hero of the Titanomachy
was made to choose first and drew the longest straw.
For his dominion he claimed the golden throne
on Mount Olympus.

For the rest, Poseidon drew the second straw.
Zeus had claimed the heavens, so Poseidon chose
to hold dominion over all the oceans.
Hades had no choice.

So it fell to him-- against his will-- to claim
the dark realm that winded deep beneath the earth:
to guard the souls of the dead after they had
met mortal judgement.

"Probable impossibilities are to be preferred to improbable possibilities."

-Aristotle

V.

Penelope Davis stood on the west side of the Acropolis in Athens, on the steps of the Propylaea. It was mid afternoon, but to the group from Olympia Heights, who were currently suffering eight hours of jet-lag, it felt like bed time. She looked down the slopes, over crumbling marble hidden between thriving olive trees, cut out against a cloudless, cyan sky. Her classmates compared trinkets from the gift shop at their last stop, but Penny was present in her setting, trying to take it all in at once.

The sound of crinkling paper snapped her out of her reverie. Minnie Rutherford, The Pantheon's very own Athena, was unfolding a map that she had picked up at information. The tour guide was busy explaining to the distracted students that *Propylaea* was plural for the Ancient Greek "porch."

"We're on the west side," Minnie said. "This is like the front step for the whole place." She folded her map carefully and handed it to Penny. "Want a map? I've memorized it."

Penny shrugged and took the map, sliding it into her black messenger bag. She set the bag on the ground and set to work on her shirt. Everyone with the school was required to wear a lime green shirt identifying them as students from Olympia Heights. It was shapeless and too large and Penny hadn't had time to hack it up in her hotel room to make adjustments. She grabbed the bottom hem, twisted, and tied a knot in the front of the shirt. "That's better."

"What are you most excited to see?" Minnie asked.

Penny shrugged. "Everything?"

Minnie smiled. "Yeah, I can see that. It's kind of like coming home, right? I can't wait to get inside the Parthenon, personally. Though this place has special significance for me, too. Did you know that in myth, Athena and Poseidon fought over this city. Guess who won?"

Penny shrugged. "You?"

"That's right."

Minnie didn't have time to recite any more history to Penny. Something, or someone, collided with her back and sent her down the last two steps of the Propylaea. She landed hard on her backside and let out a loud "Son of a--!"

It was Peter. He was scrambling to get up and help Penny up all at the same time. A group of seniors just up the steps from them were laughing and covering their mouths with the backs of their hands. One of them bumped fists with his friend.

Minnie glared daggers at them. They continued to laugh, unthreatened by the nerdy little goddess. There were four of them, one a short, freckly redhead, another a tall, skinny hispanic boy, and two who were blonde and shaped like Abercrombie models. They looked like twins, but they were not.

Minnie walked toward them. The group of boys, all players on the soccer team, exchanged glances and smirks.

"You Goth Boy's personal protector?" the short one asked. "What are you, five nothing?"

"Five four," she said, barely looking up to meet his gaze.

"I'm so scared," the skinny one said with a falsetto whimper.

"And I play roller derby."

"What's that?" Blondie number one asked.

Minnie laughed and glanced back at Peter and Penny. Peter just looked at the ground.

"You ever seen that Drew Barrymore movie where the girls knock each other around on skates?"

"Uh, yeah. Bunch-a dykes." The blondes high-fived.

Minnie ignored them. "I knock down girls twice your size and keep skating. Peter's my friend, leave him alone."

"Yeah, okay, whatever." The skinny one turned his back to Minnie.

Minnie turned around, ready to rejoin Penny and Peter. She muttered something that her friends couldn't hear.

Then something changed. Their grins vanished and they tensed.

Minnie rolled her eyes and bent down to offer Peter a hand. He had succeeded in picking Penny up, but had not made it to his feet, yet.

"What did you tell them?" Peter asked. He grit his teeth as he took her hand and pulled himself to his feet.

Minnie smiled. "That we were both friends with Frank the Tank."

"Everything alright?" Lewis asked, coming down the steps to meet them. Astin, Evan, Nick, and Teddy followed. The poor tour guide, standing above the class, knew she was being ignored.

"Just some jerks," Penny said.

Diana noticed that her brother had left his spot and met up with The Pantheon at the base of the steps. The tour guide stopped talking and Candice Matthews started taking roll... again.

"You want me to knock them around?" Nick asked, winking at Penny.

Minnie shook her head. "Bad idea, Nick. Though not the worst you've ever had, by far."

The group fell to whispers at the back of the crowd. "Have you remembered anything yet?" "Where do you think Olympus is? Literally on top of Olympus?" "Yeah, because mountain climbers over the last three thousand years never have found it." "Is anyone else cold?"

The class began to move. Minnie prodded Lewis with her finger and he started to climb the steps. The tour guide was back to chatting away in her sweet southern accent. She was blonde and perky, but not so fake that she couldn't shoot a death glare at an overzealous teenager when she heard their inappropriate comment. Minnie listened closely, memorizing everything she said.

"This particular structure was built at the conclusion of the Persian war in the 430's, BCE. It was commissioned by Pericles, who you all may remember from your World History books... No?"

Penny looked at the scaffolding that held the crumbling structure together. It wasn't bad, she thought, for a marble and limestone structure to look this recognizable after more than two thousand years.

They reached the top of the steps and the class passed through a row of six Doric columns. They were simple in design, but monumental in scale. Penny looked up as she passed under them, and when she looked down, she received quite a shock.

Everyone was gone.

Well, not everyone. Peter and Minnie stood beside her.

"Where are we?" Minnie asked.

"I don't know," Peter said.

Everyone else, the tourists, their classmates, the tour guide, were gone. The room they stood in did not look like the crumbling ruin they had been approaching, and when Penny look back through the arches, she saw nothing but billowing clouds and bright sunny sky below. The Acropolis was gone.

"Woah, shit!" Lewis appeared through the arch, nearly walking into Peter. He walked backwards on his heels, turning quickly to take in his surroundings. "We're *not* in Kansas anymore."

"Like you've ever been to Kansas, Lewis," Minnie said, shaking her head. "But allusions aside, we're clearly not at the Acropolis, either."

The others followed shortly. Soon they were all spinning around on the marble floor, taking in their surroundings and shouting profanity.

"Where is this?" Nick asked.

"Dunno," Peter said.

Nick looked at the archway, biting his lip as he thought about it. He took a deep breath and stepped back through the columns. He vanished. Diana shouted and ran to the edge, looking down, expecting to see Nick plummeting to his death. Nick stepped back in and collided with her, knocking them both to the ground.

"Where did you go?" Astin ran forward to pull Nick off of his sister. Nick seemed to be enjoying the view a little too much.

"Back to the Proppy-whatever place. It's like a portal!"

It was Astin's turn to look back over the edge. "It looks like clouds to me. Clouds and a death drop."

"Naw," Nick dusted off his shoulders. "It's like a wormhole or something, it just brings you back to the steps."

"So why did we go through it, and no one else?" Peter asked.

"Well, it's likely because of who we are, wouldn't you say?" Minnie shrugged.

They all turned to examine the place where they had arrived. Wherever the portal had brought them, it was clearly nothing any archaeologists had ever uncovered on Nat Geo. The floors were made of flawless white marble and the ceiling, also marble, was at least fifty feet high, held up with columns covered in pure gold. The room they stood in was long, and at the far end, at least a hundred yards away, sat a gold basin on a marble pedestal. The sides of the pedestal were painted in red and black with scenes of a man drinking from the basin and others of him neck-deep in water and reaching with his teeth to bite an apple just out of reach.

Around the pedestal, on three sides, was another level six inches higher than the floor. To the left and right were five thrones each with elaborate metalwork and straight ahead were two more.

Lewis dashed ahead of the group and immediately found the throne that belonged to him. The high back of the chair was made of gold and shaped like a lyre and the seat was ivory, carved to look like the underbelly of a tortoise. The arm rests were wrapped with a golden serpent. The sides of the back, at the ends of the arms of the lyre, had wings mounted on them, straight and angled for high-speed flight. Lewis sprawled across the thrones as if it were an old arm chair and spread his arms.

"Boys and girls," he said, "I think we're home."

The rest of The Pantheon jogged to catch up.

Behind the thrones was a balcony. Minnie passed right by her throne-- decorated with shields and spears, with an owl's wings sheltering the head and a olive tree made of bronze forming the back-- and looked down over the balcony. Below the throne room stretched a city made of bronze. It was empty and silent.

"This is totally Olympus," Penny said. "I've seen it in a dream. This is our throne room. That's Zach's chair, and June..." Penny knew that she had no seat here. Her own throne was in the underworld where Peter-- Hades had taken her.

Nick was standing over the basin, looking down. "What is this stuff?" he asked, pointing at the liquid it contained. The basin was filled with an opalescent liquid with a green tint.

Minnie turned back from the balcony and walked around the pedestal. She took her time examining the images painted there before nodding. "Nectar."

"What?" asked Peter.

"It's Nectar. See, this painting tells the story of Tantalus, who stole the sacred Nectar from Olympus and how he was punished for it. These are warnings, like a curse on an Egyptian tomb. Don't drink this if you're not a god or we'll punish you."

"What is Nectar?" Lewis asked. "Like from flowers?"

"Well, as usual, I'm going from myth here, so it could be wrong."

"What does the myth tell you?" Astin asked.

Minnie reached into the basin and dipped her finger in the liquid. "It's a drink that gives you eternal life." She touched the tip of her finger to her tongue and tasted the Nectar. Her eyes closed and she sighed.

"What does it taste like?" Diana asked.

"I don't know," Minnie said. "Like... a backyard barbecue with my dad."

Lewis scowled, "The Nectar of the gods tastes like barbecue sauce?"

"No. It tastes like that feeling. Like summer and family and good food."

Nick reached over Minnie's shoulder and dipped his finger in to the Nectar. As soon as he had tasted it, his lips spread into a devilish grin. "It tastes like skinny dipping at sunset on the beach. With a hot girl."

Teddy laughed and high-fived Nick. "Sweet." He reached into his bag and pulled out a shot glass that he had bought at a gift shop earlier that day. Teddy dipped it into the basin and drank. A peaceful expression washed over his face. He opened his mouth to speak, and froze.

"What?" Peter asked. "What is it?"

"Eating root beer barrels in a tree at my parents' vineyard in California."

"I have to try this," Lewis said, snatching Teddy's shot glass from his relaxed hand. He pushed Minnie aside and dipped the shot glass pack in the basin. Lewis drank.

Everyone from The Pantheon took turns drinking from the basin and telling what they felt. While everyone was interrogating Evan on his insights, Peter scooped up a bit of Nectar with his empty water bottle and saved it for later. He just didn't think he had a happy enough memory to relate it to. What if it didn't taste good for him? He didn't want everyone watching while he drank.

Evan was being practical. He held up his wrist, showing off his silver watch. "Guys, we've been here for ten minutes. You think the tour might be missing us?"

"Oh, crap, you're right!" Lewis said.

Nick rolled his eyes. "Who cares? We're on Mount Olympus, for Christ's sake! We're gods! Nobody gives a damn about the school."

"What about my Mom?" Penny asked. "You don't think she'll be a little worried?"

Lewis opened his backpack and pulled out a water bottle. He dumped the contents on the marble floor and tossed it to Evan, who barely caught it. "Fill 'er up, Evan. We'll take some back for the rest. Penny is right. We've got to move."

"Who put you in charge?" Nick asked.

"Give it a rest, Nick" Minnie said. "It's always about who's in charge with you! How about who's right? This is really cool and I'd love a chance to explore the whole city, but people are going to be looking for us and I, for one, do not want to be drawing attention to our group. In case you've forgotten, we've been responsible for a few dead bodies in the last year. I'd like to keep a low profile."

Nick mumbled something.

"Speak up or shut up." Minnie pushed past him and started off across the hall. The others followed. "When we exit through the portal, stick close to a column. We're less suspicious if we come out from behind a column, rather than appearing smack dab in the middle of nothing.

Minnie waited as each member of The Pantheon stepped beyond the columns and vanished, returning back to the steps of the Acropolis. Nick was the last to step through. Minnie put her hand out to stop him.

"What?" he asked, sticking his tongue against his cheek and refusing to look her in the eye.

Minnie stepped close. Nick towered over her, but somehow, that didn't matter. Her eyes swirled with silver fury. "When Zach's not here, I am in charge."

Nick's brow twitched in shock at the shifting of her eyes. He pulled himself together and scoffed. "Whatever."

Minnie watched him walk through the portal and followed close behind him. Dr. Davis was waiting for them on the steps.

"Where did you all go?" she asked, keeping her voice hushed but harsh.

"See those two columns?" Lewis pointed back with his thumb. "Some kind of wormhole."

"What?"

Minnie shook her head at Lewis. She stepped in front of him so she could whisper to Celene. "Basically, what he means is, we have to figure out how to catch up to the class without taking a portal to Mount Olympus."

"What?" Celene asked again.

"The short of it, for now, is that we shouldn't be walking between those two columns," Minnie said. "We'll tell you the rest at the hotel."

"I will reveal to you a love potion, without medicine, without herbs, without any witch's magic; if you want to be loved, then love."

-Hecaton of Rhodes

vi.

The occasion for the great celebration
was the marriage of mighty Zeus to Hera.
All of The Pantheon was in attendance
for the wedding feast.

A golden throne was brought forth to match the King's,
as great the couple was seated side-by side,
a tree erupted from the ground and blossomed:
a gift from the earth.

From the tree that Gaia gave them, there sprouted
a perfect crop of gleaming golden apples.
It was a great blessing for their wedding day,
a day of pure bliss.

"No better thing befalls a man than a good wife, no worse thing than a bad one."

-Semonides of Amorgos

VI.

It hadn't been easy, scraping together a short-notice wedding on a Monday afternoon. On the way into town Sunday night, June had tracked down a minister who did weddings out of a tiny chapel in Savannah, Georgia. They got in well after dark and went straight to sleep, preparing to wake up early the next day to handle paperwork.

Zach and June filled out all the forms, showed two types of identification, and even paid the extra fees for not going through a marriage course. Eight hours and one sassy courthouse clerk later, they were standing before a minister, witnessed only by the minister's wife and an elderly assistant.

The chapel was small with painted hardwood floors and simple, block, stained-glass windows. The minister's wife had hung white Christmas lights from the rafters. They twinkled like stars above them. The evening sun pouring in through those windows cast squares of colorful light on June's tea-length white dress. Zach wore his charcoal grey suit with a white tie they had picked up earlier that day. The rings had also been found that day at a pawn shop.

As June repeated the last words of her vows, she slid the simple gold band on Zach's finger. "...for as long as we both shall live," she said.

"We're married," Zach said, flipping open his wallet to find the key card for their hotel room. He missed the lock with the card as he stared at June. They had run from his Roadster to their hotel room through a light rain shower and her hair, styled that afternoon with gentle curls, lay flat and wet against her back.

"We are," she said, reaching around him to take the card and unlock the door. He was obviously too distracted, staring at the droplets of rain that beaded on her shoulders. Zach ran his knuckles along her arm.

"I can't believe we drove all the way to Savannah and got married."

"Do you regret it?" she asked as the lights on the door blinked green and she turned the doorknob.

Zach shook his head. "No." He laughed. "Not one bit." Zach pushed the door open and pressed his body against June, pinning her to the wall in the hallway at the front of their room. He kissed her, sliding his hand along her jaw and burying his fingers in her wet hair. June seemed surprised, but only for a moment now. She was married and she reminded herself that there was nothing anyone could say about her if she gave into Zach now. She was his wife. She had every right to be in this position.

June's hands gripped the lapels of his soaked suit jacket and pushed them over his shoulders. She grabbed his tie and pulled him back down to her level. Zach was officially, legally hers. It was time to let her hair down.

Zach's phone rang silently in his pocket. Eight missed calls that day. All from Dr. Jason Livingstone.

"Most men are within a finger's breadth
of being mad."

-Diogenes

vii.

In the deepest woods of the wildest regions,
a towering inferno blazed in the night.
Drunken women who had abandoned their homes
danced around the flames.

This was a temple built beneath the heavens
without stone walls or doors to keep people out.
This was the place where they went to worship him:
King of Revelry.

And when a beast would wander into their church
they would pounce upon it and tear it to bits
as an offering for the beautiful god,
great Dionysus.

"For the things we have to learn before we can do them, we learn by doing them."

-Aristotle

VII.

The hotel the school had reserved did not feel like an American hotel. It was a narrow building that sat right at the edge of the street. You could spit over the black iron railings on the balcony and hit a passing taxi. Many of the students had.

The tiled bathrooms were small and so were the rooms reserved for the students. There was no headboard, only twin lamps mounted over each bed on the wall that was half-white and half-black with paneling. Each room had a pair of double beds with bright coral comforters and a small tube television.

Tuesday evening, after a day of walking in the National Archaeological Museum and dinner outside of a café, the students were back in their rooms. Lewis and Peter had sneaked down to the room that Penny shared with Minnie. Minnie and Lewis were in the bathroom, rinsing out hotel shampoo bottles. They knew their only hope of getting the nectar from the throne room back to the states was in FAA approved miniature toiletry bottles. "Everyone takes the shampoo from their hotel," Lewis said. "No one will even think twice about it."

Monday had been a late night. With jet lag and the day of walking up hills and crumbling stone steps, none of The Pantheon had been too animated. Tonight, however, they had turned in early and had energy to spare.

"Guys!" Teddy came tearing down the hall. A maid shouted after him in Greek, something he could only assume was a command to stop running.

He stepped into the girls' room and closed the door. Nick, who Teddy was sharing a room with, banged on the door. "Hey, you locked me out."

Teddy opened the door and let Nick inside. When the door was closed, Teddy jumped up on one of the beds to make his speech. His head almost touched the ceiling.

"I, brilliant and cunning, put a piece of tape over the catch on the back door while a bellhop was out there smoking."

"So?" Penny asked.

"So? We have a way out the back door without going past reception. We can sneak out!" Teddy started dancing on the bed. "Who wants to partay?"

Nick shoved Teddy, who fell off the bed and rolled on the floor.

Someone knocked on the door. "What's going on in there?" Mrs. Matthews called through the door. "Open this door. The door needs to stay open if there are boys in here."

"Nosy b--" Nick started, but Minnie jabbed him in the side with her elbow on the way to the door.

"Let's not make her any more angry, Nick."

Minnie opened the door and smiled. "I'm sorry, Mrs. Matthews. Teddy was showing us stupid human tricks and fell off the bed when you knocked."

Candace Matthews, the frizzy-haired English teacher who was sweet on Jason Livingstone, poked her head in the room and looked around. Her gaze lingered on Penny for a moment before continuing its sweep of the room. "What is Mr. Mercer doing in there?" she asked, pointing to the bathroom.

"Washing my hands. I hear you get diarrhea really easily in foreign countries," Lewis said.

Mrs. Matthews flushed. "Keep this door open," she said.

"Yes m'am," Peter added.

"Bed check in thirty minutes. You might want to head up to your floor, boys."

After Mrs. Matthews left, Lewis came out of the bathroom, carrying a stash of shampoo bottles in the bottom of his shirt. "Everyone takes two. Don't mix them up with actual shampoo. Zach won't appreciate it if he misses Greece *and* we feed him soap."

They each took their bottles and stuffed them in pockets or luggage.

"Alright," Lewis said. He grabbed Peter by the arm and yanked him to his feet. "Ladies. We'll be back."

"What?" Penny asked.

Lewis pushed Nick out the door and looked back over his shoulder. "We have to be there for bed check. Then we'll be back."

"Guys--" Minnie started to say that this was a terrible idea. Lewis cut her off.

"Stop worrying, Mins. Live a little. See you at ten-thirty." Lewis winked and shut the door. Minnie and Penny heard the boys laughing as they ran up the hall to the elevator.

viii.

The child-god Hermes took up the dead tortoise
and with a silver scoop, he carved out its shell.
He stretched an ox skin over its hollow side
and let the hide dry.

Next he fastened on two segments of bamboo
and tied a third of the same as a crosspiece.
He strung the frame with the guts of a heifer:
a new instrument.

When he strummed the strings of his new invention,
The satyrs about him all began to dance.
None had ever heard such a beautiful sound.
It soothed their spirits.

So when Hermes fell in a spot of trouble
for the thievery of the sun god's cattle,
the tortoise shell lyre became a perfect bribe
to please Apollo.

"Not what we have, but what we enjoy, constitutes our abundance."

-Epicurus

VIII.

There was a knock on the girls' door just after ten-thirty.

"Is it them?" Minnie asked. She was in the bathroom, changing out of her pajamas from bed-check and back into a fitted t-shirt and jeans.

Penny stretched on her toes to look through the peep hole. It was Lewis. He wore a pair of black cargo shorts and a white Hawaiian shirt with a white texture palm tree print. It was as dressy as Lewis got without going to a funeral.

Minnie slipped her shirt on and went to her luggage. "Alright," she said, "Answer it."

"Good evening, ladies," Lewis said. "The boys are waiting by the ice machine on the first floor. Are you ready?"

"This is a terrible idea," Minnie said.

"Then don't come and see what trouble we get up to without your supervision." Lewis said.

They joined the boys on the first floor. Evan, Astin, Lewis, Peter, and Teddy were dressed for a night on the town. Evan wore a black collared shirt and a pair of brown dockers. As always, Teddy wore purple (tonight it was purple skinny jeans and a white polo). Astin wore a leather jacket, jeans, and an Alabama Shakes t-shirt. For Peter, dressing up meant a simple black t-shirt and a pair of jeans that fit.

"Where are Nick and Diana?" Evan asked.

"Diana has a mortal roomie," Astin said. "That girl, Alexis, from track. She decided not to risk it."

"Boo," Teddy said. "What a downer."

"Well..." Astin started, but shrugged off the end of his thought. Astin and Diana hadn't been too friendly the last six months. Diana was still grieving, and she hadn't forgotten that Astin had basically murdered her boyfriend.

"And Nick?" Minnie asked.

"He said he had other plans," Teddy said with a shrug. "I didn't ask. Probably got some kinky European porn."

Penny wrinkled her nose. "Gross."

Astin had his guitar strapped across his back, and he took out his cell phone to film himself.

"What are you doing?" Peter asked.

"It's for my Youtube channel. A hundred thousand followers. I need to upload a video this week."

"Does your phone get service here?" Peter asked.

Astin rolled his eyes and stopped recording. "No, but Wi-Fi is the same everywhere."

"Actually," Evan said, "they are slightly different standards, but most devices support bo--"

"Alright. If someone's late, they missed out. Let's go," Lewis said.

The latch to the emergency exit had been blocked by Teddy's piece of tape. They pushed it open, avoiding the bar that would set off the alarms, and wandered out into the alley.

"So, where are we going?" Teddy asked.

Lewis pointed. Up the street from their hotel, a line was forming for a club. "That looks like the place to be in Athens tonight."

The Pantheon got in line. Around them, young twenty-somethings in club wear checked their faces in compact mirrors and chatted to each other. Penny could tell that she was under-dressed in her black denim skirt, pink tights, and black screen-printed t-shirt. "I wish you had given us a better idea of what to wear," she said to Lewis, who hadn't exactly dressed for his own plans.

"It'll be fine," he said. He stepped up to the door man. "Hey," he said.

The doorman shook his head. "We have a dress code."

"Oh, come on," Lewis said. "We're only in town for a few days. We want to spend some money and have a good time."

He shook his head and stuck his thumb out, gesturing for them to step out of line.

The group gathered together.

"We could buy some new clothes?" Teddy whispered.

"You could buy new clothes," Peter said. "I'm broke."

Minnie added, "And retail won't be open at this hour."

"This can't be the only club in town. Come on," Lewis said. He waved at the door man. "Hey, thanks anyway, buddy."

Lewis started down the street. The others followed. Lewis was gone for an instant. He reappeared ahead of them in under a second and a breeze whipped around the crowd. "What the--?" the doorman said, somewhere behind them.

"What did you do?" Astin asked.

Lewis clapped his hands together, dusting them off. He pointed to a restaurant sign across the street that had been smudged by someone's hand. "I put a chalky handprint on the back of his black t-shirt. Guy was a douche."

"He was just doing his job," Evan said.

"Well his job was to be a douche."

Celene returned to her hotel room after bed check. She had taken the first half of the boys' floor. After getting visual confirmation that each of the boys was in his own room and that nobody was hiding in the bathroom, she had gone to get a bottle of water from the vending machine.

As Celene slid her key card through the lock on her door, Candice Matthews stopped at the door to the room next to her. "Having a good trip?" Celene asked. She was trying to be friendly, despite the fact that Candice had been nothing but cold to her since she'd become involved with Jason Livingstone.

Candice Matthews nodded. "It's a very nice city. The kids are having fun."

Celene nodded. She wished she had said "goodnight" instead of asking a question that had the potential to turn into an awkward conversation. "Penny does seem to be having fun," Celene said. Maybe she could end it here.

"A little too much fun, perhaps. Be careful."

Celene raised an eyebrow. "Oh?"

"That Mercer boy was in her bathroom not too long before bed check, and there was a lot of loud stumbling around before I came in."

Celene had a hard time imagining anything elicit going on in the hotel room while Minnie was there. She nodded her head. "Well, thank you for the warning, but I've been a mother long enough to know that teenagers being noisy is nothing suspicious. It's when they get quiet that you should worry."

"Hmm," Candice said.

Celene opened her door and entered her room. She threw her key card down on the night stand and collapsed on her salmon-colored bed.

Penny had visited her room before bed last night and had filled Celene in on their mysterious disappearance at the Acropolis. She knew about the nectar and about the throne room.

Lewis didn't seem like natural company for Penny or Minnie. Celene sat up. She got the sudden feeling that maybe Candice wasn't just being paranoid. Maybe something else was going on.

Celene took her key card and left the room. She walked up the hall to Penny's room and knocked. No answer.

"Nobody home?" a voice asked. Celene spun around to find Nick leaning against the wall behind her.

"Nick! What are you doing on this floor? You should be in your room."

"Yeah, and so should Teddy, but he's out for the night."

"Out? Nick, where did they go?"

Nick shrugged. "Dunno. Don't really care. But, I suppose, if you're curious, we could go look."

Celene lowered her voice. "How many of them left?"

Nick shrugged, "It sounds like Lewis was planning a Pantheon party. I didn't feel like hanging out with Minnie, though. She's been really on my case this week. Thinks she's the new Zach."

"So all of them, then? The whole Pantheon just walked out of this hotel?"

Nick leaned in close. He whispered, "One of the employees sneaked out back to have a smoke and Teddy taped the door.

Celene rubbed her eyes. "They're going to draw all sorts of bad attention to us."

"Well, then, let's go find them before they cause trouble." Nick rubbed his hands together. He was all-too-eager to get Minnie into trouble.

"No, you're going back to your room, Nick. I'm not walking out of here with a student."

"I could always go and get Ms. Matthews for you."

Celene shook her head. "No. That won't do. Just show me that back door and keep your thoughts to yourself."

Nick grinned. "My pleasure."

They were admitted easily enough at the second night club they tried. The bouncer seemed more concerned with filling the club with attractive young people than checking to make sure everyone was legal to drink in public. This place, which was lit up with neon and black lights, had a much looser dress code than the club next to the hotel. There was a DJ up on stage. All around them, people were wearing glow stick bracelets and holding brightly-colored drinks.

"Think I could get a mixed drink here?" Teddy asked.

"The drinking age is eighteen," Minnie said.

"So... yes?"

"You're not eighteen," Minnie said.

"I know." Teddy smiled and walked away.

Minnie and Penny went to find a table. The DJ shifted the music to a trance beat as someone walked on stage. They reached down and flicked a switch and an array of lasers came up from the floor and fanned out. The crowd fell quiet and the DJ made an announcement.

"What are they doing?" Astin asked as he slid into a seat at their table. Evan followed behind him with a glass of cola. He sat down and began to pick lint-- all too visible under black light-- off of his Iron Maiden shirt.

"I think it's some kind of laser harp," Minnie said.

The DJ switched tracks to some kind of accompanying music. It had bass and a beat, but no real melody. The man who had turned on the lasers shook his hands to loosen them up and then started to play. He struck each note by covering a single strand of laser light with a cupped hand. The lasers, which were every color of the rainbow, lit up the palms of his hands as he played.

"I think this is the theme from Tetris," Evan said.

"I think this is the coolest thing I've ever seen!" Astin said.

They watched as he moved through a list of songs. The rest of The Pantheon crowded around their tables. Evan took a pen and a miniature notebook out of his pocket mid-way through the set and started drawing out plans to recreate the instrument.

When the laser harp player took a bow, the crowd cheered. The DJ switched back into a club remix as the harp powered down and the musician left the stage.

"That is the best idea ever! I want one!" Astin was jumping around, energized with the possibilities of making music with this space-aged instrument.

Evan held up the napkin. "I can make one."

"Really?"

"Really. When we get home. Of course, supplies will cost a little."

"You are the best!" Astin grabbed the sides of Evan's head. "Evan, if you build me that thing, I will owe you forever!"

Teddy stood up. "Alright, who wants shots?" he asked. "I'm paying."

Celene approached the doorman with the big chalk handprint on his shirt. He looked at Nick, dressed in a polo and khakis, then looked down at the Crocs on his feet, and shook his head. "Dress code," he said.

"That's okay," Celene said. "We're not looking to come in. We're just wondering if you've seen a group of students. They're all between fifteen and eighteen."

"I see a lot of students," he said. It was clear from his perfect English that he was very used to dealing with tourists.

"This one had a smart-mouthed kid with blonde hair," Celene said. She opened her wallet and held up a photo of Penny. "And this girl."

The bouncer nodded. "They didn't meet dress code, so I sent them on their way. There's one other club in walking distance that allows jeans and trainers, if you go down to the next cross street and take a left, you can't miss it."

"Thanks," Celene said. "Really, thank you, Sir."

"Good luck," he said, before turning back to his line.

Lewis sat at the bar, sipping from a glass of tonic water. He thought he might be able to get a drink here, but he wanted to keep his wits sharp. His mind was buzzing with ideas for mischief. Already the novelty of sneaking into a night club was wearing thin.

A woman sat at the bar next to him. She was probably in her late twenties with dark hair and olive skin. Lewis leaned closer to her. "So what is there to do in this city after hours?"

She glanced sideways at him, "Eh... no English."

"Ah," Lewis sat up straight in his bar stool. "Sorry. Uh..." Lewis searched his brain for the few phrases of Greek he had learned before the trip. "Signommi," he added.

A man seated on the other side of him tapped his shoulder.

"Are you looking for a good time?"

Lewis looked the man over. "Sorry, dude. You're too old for me."

The man handed Lewis a poker chip. "Buy-in tonight is only fifty Euro."

Lewis took the chip and flipped it across his knuckles. "Thanks, man." He flipped the chip into the air and caught it. His eyes settled on Minnie, and he knew what he wanted to do. "Really, thanks."

Minnie pushed her way through the crowd, heading towards the bar. She needed a glass of water. It was too hot and crowded in the club for comfort.

She spotted Teddy's purple skinny jeans at the bar. Minnie slid into the stool next to him. Teddy was receiving a drink at the bar, something that looked, to Minnie's inexpert eyes, like Sangria. The bartender pointed to a man across the bar. He was young, probably only two years older than Teddy, and he smiled and waved.

"Can't buy your own drinks?" Minnie asked.

"He doesn't need to know I'm filthy rich. It's the gesture that counts." Teddy took a long sip of his drink. "They skimp on the booze at this bar."

Minnie looked between the man and Teddy, confused. Was Teddy playing him for free liquor?

Teddy leaned in close and whispered. "Stop looking so lost, Minnie. I'm bisexual."

"Oh," she said, blinking. That shouldn't have come as a surprise, she thought. She was very familiar with his mythological past. "Does anyone else know?"

"A few people at school. Certainly not my mom. My dad's a Senator. A Republican Senator. It wouldn't be well accepted if it came out that his son was... fluid."

"Well, your secret's safe with me. Just be careful. Greece isn't as accepting as the rest of Western Europe."

Lewis ran up to the bar, nearly knocking Minnie off of her stool. "Minnie, I need you."

"This is a dramatic confession," Teddy teased.

"So not what I meant. Come on." He grabbed her hand and pulled her down. "We have work to do."

Minnie looked confused, but she decided to follow Lewis rather than cause a scene in front of the curious bartender. "I'll see you later, Teddy. Be careful."

"Teddy!" Lewis said, suddenly remembering something. "Can we borrow a hundred bucks?"

"Dare I ask?"

Lewis grinned manically.

Teddy shook his head and pulled out his wallet. He handed a hundred Euro to Lewis and waved him off. "Now go, before he thinks I'm with one of you."

The Blood of Athens

"Where are we going?" Minnie asked.

"You'll find out. It's brilliant!"

"Live today, forget the past."
-Greek Proverb

ix.

After the delivery of the infant,
the mother took flight from her Godly lover.
The father, Lord Apollo, was heartbroken
and left with his son.

Coronis had fallen in love with Ischys,
so she abandoned baby Asclepius,
putting her happiness over her own son--
a most selfish deed.

Apollo's sister, Artemis, was enraged,
and she followed Coronis and her lover.
In the faintest moonlight she entered their home
and slit both their throats.

Artemis never told this to her brother,
but instead let her vengeance pass in silence.
She returned to his side to help raise his son
as a loyal aunt.

"Begin with your own family."
-Lykurgus

IX.

"Zach, pick up your phone. I haven't been able to get a hold of you or June since Sunday. We need to talk. It's important." Jason hung up after leaving his seventh voicemail for Zach. He was on his way back from the dentist with his kids. An unfamiliar car sat in his driveway. Jason examined the gold Lexus as he stepped out of his car. South Carolina plates. The only people he knew in South Carolina were--

"Jason!" his father shouted from the doorstep. Of course, Paul Livingstone bought a new car every two years like clockwork. Jason glanced back at the gold Lexus and sighed with relief. After Sunday's meeting with Mr. Spade, Jason had expected the worst.

"Has it been two years yet?" Jason asked.

His father shrugged. "Close enough."

Jason's aunt came around the front of the house from the side yard. She had gone to retrieve the spare key from the planter outside the kitchen window. Haley shouted, "Aunty Liza!" as she ran towards the silver-haired woman.

Jason and his father shared the same crinkly eyes and sturdy jaw line. While Jason's hair was brown with a mix of silver, his father's hair was now a brilliant white. Paul Livingstone was seventy-two. He and his sister, Elizabeth, had raised Jason. Paul and Elizabeth were twins. Jason's mother had run off with another man shortly after his birth.

"How are my boys?" Paul asked, as Jason unbuckled Jamie from his car seat.

"I wasn't expecting you, Dad."

"Yeah, well, Joe Lowenstein passed away. You remember him? The snowbird with the loud wife? We had to drive down for the funeral-- plane tickets on this notice cost a small fortune-- so we decided to swing east forty minutes to see you. Hope I'm not interrupting anything. Plans with the girlfriend?" He cocked an eyebrow.

"Celene is in Athens with the school trip," Jason said.

"We were hoping to finally meet her," Aunt Elizabeth said, disappointed. She was already busy braiding Haley's hair.

"She won't get back until later this week. How long are you in town?"

"Just for the night," she said. "We plan to hit the road tomorrow after lunch."

They all headed into the house. Jason had been planning on baking a pizza for dinner. Luckily, the pizzas had been buy-one-get-one when he'd last gone shopping. He preheated his oven.

Jason left his father and his aunt in the kitchen and took the kids into the living room. He started up Netflix and signed the kids in to the children's channel. Haley and the twins settled down on the overstuffed sofa to watch cartoons. Jason rejoined the adults at the kitchen table.

"Of course, it would have to be okay with Jason," his aunt said.

"What has to be okay with me?"

"Your aunt wants to get Haley an iPad for her birthday. I told her kids don't need all of that technology. Especially not something that expensive."

"Oh they aren't that bad. I'm not going to get her one with 3G for God's sake."

Paul grumbled and got up to check the refrigerator.

"Jesus, Jason, this thing is barren."

"It's been a busy weekend. I haven't gone for groceries yet."

"Oh, don't worry," Elizabeth said with a gentle smile. "Paul, sit down. Jason can just make some tea. You do have tea, right dear?"

Jason nodded and got up from the table.

"I was really looking forward to meeting your girlfriend. It's been so long since you've seen anyone."

"You should have gone on that trip," Paul said. "We could've taken Haley and the twins. We didn't do so bad with you, you know."

"Yes, well, there weren't enough slots for chaperones," he said. In reality, Jason didn't want to leave so close to Devon's due date. That, and he didn't want to be stuck on a plane with Candice Matthews, even if Celene was there as a buffer.

"That's alright," Elizabeth said. "You can go on a trip with just the lady friend now. I can't imagine it's very romantic, supervising teenagers."

Jason laughed and shook his head. "No," he said, rinsing the tea kettle and drying the outside. "That's not exactly what I'd call a vacation.

It was quiet while Jason put the kettle on and got the sugar and creamer out.

"I got a funny message from one of my old residents on the Facebook yesterday," Paul finally said.

"Oh yeah?" Jason rummaged through the cabinets to find a choice of herbal teas. He returned to the table to an armful of half-empty cardboard boxes.

"She says she saw you at the hospital Sunday? Says you're playing doctor to some pregnant teenagers?" It was clear from his tone that he was just waiting for Jason to say she was mistaken. Jason had to wonder if he had really diverted forty minutes for a visit or if it was for a lecture.

"Uh... yeah. That's about right." Jason had no idea how to explain the situation to his father. "She's one of the kids from the school. She came to me first when she was pregnant."

"Jason, you haven't really practiced medicine in years, and you were never an obstetrician."

"I just helped her get prenatal vitamins and balance her diet. She needed someone she trusted," Jason said.

"Did you at least bring her to a hospital for prenatal screening?"

"Yes," Jason lied. Devon had refused to see another doctor. They knew that when it came time to deliver, there was no hiding the baby, but Devon hadn't wanted anyone to find out if something was abnormal until after she'd delivered.

"Why you didn't just refer her to an O.B.G.Y.N is beyond me."

"It's complicated. I can't explain. You know, confidentiality."

Jason's father eyed him suspiciously. He opened his mouth to speak, but was cut off.

"I was hoping to meet your girlfriend," Elizabeth said, rescuing Jason from further scolding. "And her daughter. You said she has a daughter, right?"

Jason nodded. "Penny. She's a sophomore in high school."

"That must be nice for Haley, to have an older girl to look up to."

"Penny's a good kid. She's got a good head on her shoulders."

"What happened to Penny's dad?" his father asked with a raised eyebrow.

"Died. Cancer."

A whistling from the tea kettle broke their conversation. Jason rushed over to pull it off the stove while his aunt rummage through the tea boxes to pick her flavor. "Ooh, rasberry zinger," she said, trying to diffuse the tension with idle chatter.

Paul Livingstone rose from his seat and retrieved three mugs from Jason's cabinets. "Just remember," he said after a long and mulled-over pause, "Haley, Jamie, and Scott. They are your top priority. I have no doubt that this woman is something special, but your kids come first."

Special. Celene and Penny were certainly special. Jason glanced over at the business card stuffed into the side of his bill basket. Mr. Spade was expecting a call. He took a deep breath and nodded. "I know, Dad."

Jason poured three mugs of hot water. As their tea brewed, he opened the frozen pizzas and put them on a cookie sheet for dinner. Family first, he reminded himself as he slid the pizzas into the oven. The Pantheon wasn't *his* family.

"We hang the petty thieves and appoint
the great ones to public office."

-Aesop

X.

The slender trickster stood before a locked door,
a metal barrier, bolted and chained shut.
As his body turned to a blanket of mist,
he smirked so slightly.

The silver cloud of mist passed through the keyhole
and reincorporated in the god's form,
standing inside the chamber without a sound,
surrounded by gold.

As he silently surveyed all this treasure
the subtle smirk transformed into a broad grin.
Moments just like these were the reason they called
him the King of Thieves.

"A lucky person is someone who plants pebbles and harvests potatoes."

-Greek Proverb

X.

"Where are we going?" Minnie asked Lewis as he dragged her down the street. They had left their friends back at the night club and were heading in an unknown direction through the streets of Athens. Lewis was on a mission.

"You ever see that movie about the Harvard card counters?"

"It's MIT, but yes."

"We're going to do that. Or rather, you're going to do that."

"So what are you here for?"

"I'm the charisma. Now, you saw the movie, so you remember it, right?"

"You mean how to play and how to count cards?"

"Yeah."

"Sure, I mean, whatever I didn't get from the movie, I clarified with a YouTube video."

Lewis clapped his hands and bounced around excitedly. "Sweet."

"This is insane," Minnie said.

"But it's a challenge. You know your wits love a challenge."

Ten minutes later, Minnie and Lewis walked through the doors of the casino. Lewis pointed to a 3:2 blackjack table with a fifty Euro minimum marked on a kelly-green sign. Lewis wasn't eighteen, but he was allowed to tag along. Minnie was the legal age to gamble, so he handed Teddy's starting money over to let her purchase chips.

Minnie, sat down at the blackjack table. "Alright, Mins," he said. "One hand. If you lose, that's it and we go back to the hotel."

"Are aces high or low?" Minnie asked, adopting a higher-pitched voice and trying to sound like Devon Valentine's cheerleader friends.

The dealer changed the cash for chips and pushed them across the table to Minnie. "Sir, I'll need to remind you not to touch the cards" he said.

Lewis tapped the betting circle in front of Minnie. "Right here, Minnie. You put your bet here."

"I know how to play," she scolded. "My father used to play me for skittles."

Lewis stepped back and slipped his hands into his pockets. "Like taking candy from a baby," he whispered.

His lips hardly moved and his voice was inaudible, but he sent his words to Minnie's ears and she heard him loud and clear.

It was a shoe game, so the dealer played everyone's hand face-up. This made it easy for Minnie to look at their cards and figure out what was left. Lewis watched as she played. In the movies, guys had to practice for weeks before the basic strategy of card counting was ingrained in them. Minnie was too smart for this. She ran the calculations in her mind, deciding almost instantly if probability was in her favor. After half an hour she had tripled their money. Lewis kept up a steady banter with the other players, telling jokes and letting a young woman ramble on about the Greek version of *Next Top Model.*

Twenty minutes later, that money was tripled again. They now had nine times the money they had walked in with. Lewis saw an official-looking man in a suit whispering to one of the security guards.

"Alright Mins," Lewis said. "Your mom's waiting for us back at the hotel."

"But I'm winning!"

"Ever hear the phrase 'quit while you're ahead'?"

Minnie finished the hand she was playing, bringing their total to an even one thousand Euros. She scooped up her chips.

"Bye," she said. "You've been great. This was so much fun."

She dumped the chips into the hem of Lewis' shirt and he carried them to the counter to cash them in. "We were getting noticed," he whispered, using his power to make sure that only Minnie could hear him. "That said, nice performance. I was surprised."

"I'm full of surprises," Minnie announced as he dumped the chips on the counter.

"So what do you say?" Lewis asked as they walked out of the casino, counting their money, "Pay Teddy back with interest?"

"Two hundred for him, two hundred for you, six hundred for me."

"Two hundred?"

"You were charming, Lew, but really, without my brain, you had nothing."

Lewis sighed. "Fair enough."

"Man's life is like a drop of dew on a leaf."
  -Socrates

xi.

The body was cleaned with water from the sea
and it was dressed in a white burial shroud.
A diadem of celery was placed on
the dead man's forehead.

He had died in battle and so he was
to be buried in his military cloak.
A strap for his chin held the coin in his mouth
for the ferryman.

They laid him out on a bed with checkered cloth
so that his feet faced the door of the bedroom.
After the ritual of lamentation
they'd burn his body.

"It is possible to provide security against other ills, but as far as death is concerned, we men live in a city without walls."

-Epicurus

XI.

"Yes," the tall bouncer said, tapping the photo in Celene's wallet with his index finger. He was dressed in a long leather coat and wore too many gold rings. "She and friends, they come in here."

"Thank you," Celene said. She tried to enter, but the bouncer stepped in her way. "We are full."

"My daughter is in this club," Celene said.

"She is grown up. She take care of her self."

"She is not a grown up," Celene hissed. "She's fifteen."

Nick put his hand on Celene's shoulder. "Come on. I have a better idea."

Nick took her wrist and pulled Celene down the street. "No offense, Dr. D, because you're a total MILF, but they wouldn't let us in because I'm just barely eighteen and you're not twenty-five anymore."

Celene wasn't sure if she should be offended or flattered. She knew what MILF stood for, after all, and it wasn't very polite.

"So how do we get in?"

Nick shrugged. "I dunno. I just didn't want you to stand in line arguing. That's embarrassing."

Celene shook her head. "Well how did they get in if they're not eighteen?"

"They've got hot girls with them. Duh. That's how night clubs work. They'll take an Evan if it gets them Penny and Minnie."

Celene scowled. "Alright. So we wait?"

"Or," Nick said, looking around at the line outside the club, "I could try to get in with one of those lovely ladies over there."

"We wait," she said, ignoring Nick's suggestion. "They have to come out some time. And when they do, I'll rip them a new one."

Lewis and Minnie pushed their way through the crowd until they had made it to the table that the rest of The Pantheon had claimed. Teddy was gesturing wildly as he told a story to Astin, Penny, and Evan.

Lewis clamped his hand over Teddy's shoulder.

"Do you have my hundred Euros?" Teddy asked.

"Plus some. We'll talk about that later. Just saw cops talking to the manager at the back. They want to close-off this joint. Time to go."

They hurried to stand up. Nobody wanted to be delayed in getting back to the hotel before they were missed.

"Where's Peter?" Penny asked.

"Taking a leak," Teddy said.

"Someone should get him."

"No problem," Lewis said. He turned his head towards the bathroom and narrowed his eyes. His lips moved as he whispered. "Got it," he finally said. "Unless he wasn't in the bathroom, but the cops were out at that end of the club, so I'm not risking my ass to drag him out of the bathroom."

Peter had spent the evening alone. He had only come along on their late-night excursion to be close to Penny, but she had spent the evening talking about music with Astin and Evan, and Peter had spent it sitting in a corner booth, invisible. At first he had let himself slip out of sight to see if anyone would notice. They hadn't. He had spent the last hour people-watching, and only had risen to use the bathroom when a couple had invaded his booth to make out.

Peter scanned over the graffiti on the door of the bathroom stall. What could he have done differently? He thought he looked good, or as good as he could look when all of his clothing came from Goodwill. His clothes fit, and wasn't black flattering on everyone? Maybe he should have flirted with other girls or sat near her and laughed at her jokes. That kind of jovial facade was just not Peter.

Peter left the bathroom stall and crossed to the sink. He turned the water on, finding that it went from freezing cold to scalding hot, and never rested anywhere in between. After a rushed hand-washing job, he pressed on the large button for the hand drier. He spotted something odd in the mirror.

The stall directly behind him was cracked open, but there were feet showing beneath the door. Peter turned and knocked. "Dude, your door is open."

No response.

"You alright?" he asked. He was a bit worried that, if he opened the door, he'd find someone passed out with their drawers down. He asked again, then gently pressed on the door, giving the occupant plenty of notice to push it closed.

The door swung open. The man sitting on the toilet was wearing clothes stained black with blood. His eyes were wide, one red with the blood of a burst capillary. He appeared to have multiple stab wounds, as well as bruising around his throat. Peter staggered back as the first drops of blood wicked through the corpse's trousers and dripped onto the tile floor. The man's mouth hung open, his tongue hanging out. Resting there was a single gold coin.

"Not again," Peter mumbled.

"It's in here," someone said, obviously American, through the door. "I just went to take a piss and there was a dead guy. You gotta call the police."

Peter ducked into another stall. He couldn't be caught with a body in the bathroom. He'd already been associated with enough suspicious deaths to last him a lifetime. Like turning off a television, Peter's image disappeared. He waited by the bathroom door, and when the manager opened it to come look, Peter slipped out behind him.

The other members of The Pantheon made their way to the front door and waited across the street. It was getting so late that it was early again, and the group knew they would be dragging on their tour tomorrow. "Where is he?" Teddy asked, tapping his foot impatiently.

"Right here," Peter said. Teddy jumped.

"Shit, don't sneak up on us like that," Teddy said, glaring at a seemingly-empty space beside him.

"Guys," Peter said, still invisible. "We need to talk."

"We sure do," Nick said. The group turned to see Nick and Dr. Davis walking up the street.

"Benedict Arnold," Lewis murmured.

"We were just about to come looking for you. You seven are in deep--" Celene started.

Peter interrupted her. "No offense, but we've got worse things to worry about."

"Peter?" Celene asked, staring at the empty space between Penny and Teddy.

"I'm this way because I had to sneak out of the bathroom," he said. "Before the police came."

Celene rolled her eyes. "What did you do?"

"Nothing," Peter said. He lowered his voice so that he was just barely audible over the sounds of late-night traffic on the busy street. "I mean, someone else did something. There was a body," he said. "There was a dead guy in the bathroom. All jacked-up."

"Cool," Nick said. "Murder in Athens."

"Wait, there's been a serial killer in the news," Minnie said.

"Yeah," Peter said, "Remember that article we read on the plane? The police said he liked to kill in public places--"

"But they never released an M.O." Minnie said.

"Right, well... it might be a total coincidence, but I'd say this guy knows his Greek history." They all waited for him to go on. "The killer left a coin in the guy's mouth."

"Coincidence or not," Celene said, "I don't want you seven seen at the scene of another murder. Let's get back to the hotel. I'll let Jason scream at you when we get home."

"A mad bull is not to be tied up with a pack thread."

    -Greek Proverb

xii.

The infants were twins, but only half-brothers.
One was the true son of their mother's husband
and the other belonged to the mighty Zeus.
The boys shared a crib.

Jealous Hera plotted to kill the bastard
and sent a pair of most poisonous serpents
to visit the infants in their crib at night.
Herakles woke up.

When their mother sensed trouble under her roof
she ran in the room to find one child sleeping
while the other child waved two strangled serpents
and gleefully laughed.

"Act when you know."
-Delphic Maxim

XII.

"We'll be in town for Haley's birthday," Elizabeth Livingstone said as she hugged her nephew. Paul Livingstone loaded their suitcases into the trunk of his Lexus while his sister fussed over Jason. "You're getting grey. Pretty soon we won't be able to tell you and your father apart."

Jason ran his fingers through the sides if his hair. "Yes, well, working with teenagers, you age quickly."

They said their goodbyes and pulled out of the driveway. Jason went inside and sat down with a fresh mug of coffee. The kids were in the living room, coloring pictures from *My Little Pony: Friendship is Magic* and eating toaster waffles.

Jason perched his mug on the ceramic coaster next to his computer and opened his email. There was an incredibly cryptic message from Celene waiting for him.

Jason,

Everyone is safe.

Celene

He chewed on the edge of his tongue as he mulled that one over. Surely Celene wouldn't send an email about just that topic unless it had some relevance in their lives. *Everyone is safe?* Was there some reason they shouldn't be?

He was just reaching for his mug of coffee when his phone vibrated in his pocket. Jason jumped out of his chair to retrieve it, hoping that it was Zach finally getting in touch with him. It was Frank.

"Frank," he said when he answered the phone. "Everything alright with the baby?"

Devon's voice spoke over her boyfriend's phone. "You need to come see this. Really."

Jason frowned. "Alright. Uh... let me call the sitter. It might take me a while. Is this an emergency?"

"Uh," Devon hesitated.

"You know what, don't tell me over the phone," Jason warned.

"Okay," Devon said. "You'll see when you get here."

Jason pulled up outside the Guerrero home forty minutes later. The house was owned by Frank's aunt, but his aunt and his mother worked days, leaving Frank and Devon alone with their new baby. Devon had only been released from the hospital the morning before, and Xander had been given a clean bill of health. What could have changed in twenty-four hours?

Frank came to the door when Jason knocked and cracked it only an inch to look outside. When he saw Jason, he rushed him inside with a very conspiratorial wave.

"What's going on?" Jason asked. "Is it... horns or something?"

Frank walked silently towards his bedroom; Jason followed.

Until a few months ago, Frank's room had been sparse with a few posters, basic furniture, and the occasional dirty sock on the floor. Devon had taken over since moving in. The walls had been repainted a sea-foam green and, mounted on the wall, was Frank's football jersey from Olympia Heights Senior High. It was framed with a photo of their team, the Olympia Thunder, gathered around the state championship photo from December of this year. Devon had thrown out Frank's tattered comforter and replaced it with the red quilt from her old bedroom. Most noticeably, the once bare room was now filled with baby toys, baby clothes, and baby books. The cheerleading team had gone overboard hosting her baby shower.

Jason crossed the room to Xander's crib. He looked down. Just Sunday morning, the infant had had thick, dark hair. Jason's own daughter, Haley, had come out of the womb with almost black hair, only to sprout blonde curls by her first birthday. But this had been three days, and what he saw now was not natural at all. Xander's hair, once thin, black, and straight, was now a thick mass of springy curls, as tight as fleece. That wasn't the extraordinary part, however. What Jason saw was impossible. The hair on that baby's head was the color of pure gold.

Xander looked up, and Jason looked back into his green-blue eyes, the same color as Devon's. "That's not normal, right?" Devon asked.

Jason shook his head. Xander smiled. "No," he said. "That's not normal. Devon, pull the blinds. Frank... do you have an electric razor?"

"You're going to shave his head?" Devon asked, alarm evident in her voice. "Is that really necessary?"

Jason tore his eyes from the infant and nodded at Devon. "It is," he said. He took a deep breath. "I've got something to tell you both. We have a new friend... Mr. Spade."

"It is of the nature of desire not to be satisfied, and most men live only for the gratification of it."

-Aristotle

xiii.

Zeus was not the only god known for his lust.
The god of the sea had as many affairs.
His desire was not confined to his marriage.
This is one such tale:

When Poseidon set his mind to seducing
Demeter, the true goddess of the harvest,
she did not reciprocate his interest,
so she fled from him.

The goddess took the form of a dappled mare,
and so Poseidon turned into a stallion,
and in like form he chased her across the earth
and overtook her.

Demeter bore an offspring from his conquest.
As they had both taken the form of horses,
their new child was a stallion, a hero's mount
they named Areion.

"Our sins are more easily remembered than our good deeds."

-Democritus

XIII.

The escapades of the night before hadn't done much to hinder the waking hours for The Pantheon. Their bodies still weren't used to the time difference between Florida and Athens anyway, and there was plenty of time to sleep on buses. They had spent the morning sleep-walking through the National Archaeological Museum, but a nap on the bus followed by the discovery of a foreign caffienated drink in a bright red can had renewed their energy.

The afternoon tour was to the Kerameikos cemetery. The enormous ancient cemetery featured low stone walls and crumbling columns that divided patches of green grass. They had walked through the museum shortly after lunch, looking at ancient pottery much like the pieces they had seen in the National Museum that morning. Red clay pots were painted with black bases and scenes of static figures enacting ancient myths. After a walk through the museum, they made their way out into the cemetery. To keep them on task, the art teacher had given them a scavenger hunt of statues to photograph.

Peter and Penny had snapped the bull on her pink camera and the lion had been directly next to it. They traveled with a group of students being chaperoned by one of the history teachers. The group had stopped to listen to Mr. McCracken read a tour pamphlet about a relief of Athena when Peter saw something just beyond the palms behind them.

"What's that hole?" he asked, leaning to whisper to the closest ear.

He had asked one of the soccer players, and the other boy looked around before saying, "What hole?"

"Uh, you know, the gaping cave mouth right behind us."

The boy kept looking before turning back to listen to Mr. McCracken. "Stop messing around, Hadley."

"I'm no--"

"Whatever. Loser." He shoved Peter's shoulder, but not hard enough to make him fall.

Peter fell back in the crowd and drifted to the left until he was standing next to Penny. He nudged her with his elbow.

"What?" she hissed, shooting him a glare. She was trying to listen.

Peter tipped his head back over his shoulder. "Look."

Penny turned around and laid eyes on the mouth of the cave. She looked back at Peter.

"Can you see it?" he whispered.

"Of course."

"Blockhead over there can't."

"What?"

Peter smirked. "Let's check it out."

The group was allowed to wander for a few minutes. They had reached the meet-up spot for the tour. "Don't leave my sight," Mr. McCracken said. "But you can take pictures and talk until the other groups catch up.

Peter approached the hole. To the others, it was just a patch of green grass with a few slabs of stacked marble laying around. To Peter and Penny, however, the ground sloped downward and dipped under the marble, which framed a doorway to a black pit below. Peter looked down into the hole. There was a path that winded inside and vanished in the dark. "I wanna go in," he said.

Penny looked down the same hole and shook her head. Just looking down it made her feel claustrophobic. She wanted to get away, but she was dying to know what was inside. "Not with everyone watching."

"It's gotta be another portal, like the one at the Acropolis," he said.

"And it goes down? Three guesses where that leads to."

Celene's group was reaching the end of the tour. She was surprised to find that Nick, the student who, last year, had been one of the worst-behaved students in her chemistry class, was helping to keep order and move things along. Her group stopped in front of the relief of Athena, and

Minnie, who Celene had surrendered the pamphlet to, told her classmates about the carving.

Celene's eyes fell on Penny and Peter. They were standing at the entrance to a cave. Celene had seen that cave in her dreams. It was a hell-mouth. It was entrance to Hades that Demeter returned to every spring to wait for her daughter. Celene abandoned her group and walked as quickly as she could across the grass.

"Penny," she hissed. "Penny. Get away from there."

Penny was staring down into the darkness and listening. She swore she could hear something below calling to her. Her mother's voice broke her out of her focus and she whirled around.

"Dr. Davis," Peter said quietly. Some of the students were watching them. "They can't see this, so take it easy."

Celene looked around at the students. Curious eyes waited for Celene to go on. She took a deep breath and wrapped her hand around Penny's arm. "Come here, I want to show you this relief."

"I've already seen it, Mom."

Celene lowered her voice to a whisper, "I don't want you near that pit."

Penny nodded. "Alright."

Peter watched Celene drag Penny away from the cave. He glanced back down into the darkness before shaking his head. He was never going to get a chance to explore with all of these eyes on him. He quietly said goodbye to the promise of answers and rejoined the tour group. It was nearly time for dinner anyway, and Peter was starving.

The Blood of Athens

When they returned to the hotel Wednesday evening after dinner, the group still had copious amounts of energy. Celene was certain that they would not escape the hotel this time, and planted herself with a book next to the lobby door.

That left them with no choice but to wander from room to room before curfew, hanging out and spending their time talking, rather than getting up to trouble.

Peter sat on the bed in Penny and Minnie's hotel room, fiddling with a metal puzzle that he had picked up at a gift shop. Penny sat on the floor, organizing a bag of brochures and tickets for scrap-booking when she returned home.

"I'm just saying, there were way too many people at The Agora for it to be fun," Peter said. "Dead and alive."

"But there was so much to see and buy."

"We cross the Atlantic Ocean to go shopping? We could do that at home."

"You can't buy that stuff at home."

"You can on the internet," Peter mumbled. "And this piece of crap. This, I could easily buy at home."

"Well that was the museum gift shop. And you only think it's crap because you can't solve it." Penny got up and walked to the bed. She took the puzzle out of Peter's hand and twisted it. In just a few moves it was in two pieces.

"How did you--?"

"I've been watching you attempt it for an hour. I got some ideas."

Peter tossed the puzzle to the foot of the bed.

"Are you going to complain about a free trip, Peter? Wasn't the Acropolis alone worth it? And I know you didn't get to go inside, but the cave at the cemetery..."

Peter sighed. "It's just not what I thought it would be."

"You expected more than walking through an archway to Mount Olympus? *And* an entrance to Hades?"

"I didn't expect to fly almost six thousand miles away from home, only to find yet another dead body."

Penny sat down next to Peter. "Oh. That."

"Yeah. That."

"We sure have found a lot of bodies, huh?" Penny tried to recall them all. First it was the guy that Diana found in the woods, then the museum curator, and did they count the Titans that they killed? Penny had helped Frank bury the body of Atlas only a few months before. "I would think you'd get used to death, what with seeing ghosts," Penny said.

"Yeah. Well a ghost and a recently offed corpse are two different things."

"Is it weird that the guy's ghost wasn't hanging around?"

Peter shrugged. "Maybe? Not all violent-deaths leave spirits behind. Maybe he was slightly suicidal. Maybe he was just extremely emotionally healthy and didn't fear death. Anyway, I didn't have time to look around. I didn't want to be found with a corpse in a bathroom overseas. American students don't exactly do well in foreign courts."

"I'm sorry, Peter."

Peter just nodded.

"Really. Anyone could have found that guy. I'm sorry it had to be you."

"It's okay. Someone from the Pantheon needed to see it. We might be in danger. Again."

"Or it's a serial killer who is really into his heritage. We are in Athens."

"True." Peter looked down at his hands. "I'm just a magnet for death."

"That's not true. Diana found that guy last fall and everyone found the museum curator together. You don't have it any worse than the rest of us."

"Penny," Peter said. "I see ghosts all the time. When I was born, I killed my mother."

Penny looked away.

"I have to blackmail my dad to keep his hands off me because he knows. He knows it's my fault."

"People die, Peter. It's not your fault. Your father doesn't have the right to hurt you because he doesn't know how to handle his own sadness."

Peter nodded. "Dr. Livingstone wants me to get emancipation and live at a shelter."

"Maybe you could live with my mom."

Peter laughed. "Your mom hates me."

"She doesn't hate you."

"She certainly doesn't want us under the same roof."

Penny didn't dispute that. "Are you going to do it?"

"I might. Doc says the blackmail isn't a long-term solution."

Penny threw her arms around his shoulders. He looked like he needed a hug. Peter buried his nose in her hair and closed his eyes, just breathing and enjoying the warmth of her embrace. Peter wasn't a particularly huggy person, but physical contact from Penny was always welcome.

As Penny pulled away, Peter felt the moment. It was that moment, when watching a romantic comedy, that every member in the audience could anticipate the big, climactic kiss. It was the right moment. He had to go for it. Peter turned his head, his lips passed by her cheek and then he was kissing her. The stars had aligned.

Penny pressed her hand to his chest and pushed him away. She stood up and turned around.

Peter's heart tightened in his chest. He opened his mouth, starting to apologize, but he didn't *want* to apologize.

"Why did you do that?" Penny asked.

"You know why," he said.

"Peter," she warned.

"I love you, and it's not just because it's been engrained in my soul for a couple thousand years. I love you, Penny, not Persephone."

"I thought we covered this in August," she said. "You're my friend."

"Why am I just your friend? Because I'm not rich like Teddy? Because I'm not as charming as Zach? Not as tall as Frank? Not as handsome as Nick?"

"How about because you raped me."

Peter fell silent for a moment. He stood up. "That wasn't me. That was Hades."

"Which is part of you." Penny sighed. "I know it doesn't seem fair, to be blamed for things that we did when--"

"No, it's not fair. I'm a different person. I was born Peter Hadley, grew up in a shitty house with my shitty dad, and I would never do that to you."

"I know."

They looked at each other for a long time. Penny had to admit that Peter had become quite tall and handsome over the last year and a half. He was her best friend, but it wasn't enough. "Peter. When you remember me, do you see me, Penny Davis?"

Peter furrowed his brow. "You mean when I remember Persephone?"

"Right."

"No. But I know it's you."

"Exactly. Like a dream. You don't look like you, but I know it's you. And when I finally remembered that, when that memory came back to me or was unlocked or whatever the hell happened, I remembered it as you. So you, Peter Hadley, never did that to me, and never would-- I hope--

but I remember it as you, because it kind of was you, before. I know this doesn't make sense, but it doesn't have to."

Penny began to cry. "When you try to kiss me, Peter, I remember being dragged through the earth and taken against my will. Nothing will ever fix that. You could look like Darren Criss and have all the money in the world, and I would still have that in my mind. I can't be with you, Peter. Ever. And I know it isn't fair, which is why you're still my best friend, but some part of you long ago is guilty, and I can't forget it, even if I've forgiven it. I can't be with someone that I fear, even a little. I can't ever forget that."

Peter sat down on the bed. He took Penny's hand. She tensed, but she didn't pull away. It had taken two years for Peter to understand. He got it now. All of this time he had worried that Penny didn't like him as a person. He was angry for being saddled with the guilt of something he had done in a past life. When he had met Penny, he hadn't felt like Hades, Lord of the dead. Now, as more memories came back, he knew that that identity was part of his life. She knew it, too. She didn't blame him. She didn't hate him. She forgave him. She just couldn't break that association.

"I'm sorry," he said.

"I know you are."

"Thank you for explaining that to me."

Penny hugged him and Peter left it at that, just a hug.

"Friends?" she asked.

Peter nodded. "Of course." Though there was a painful twisting in his gut, Peter understood. It wasn't fair, but he couldn't fix it. Trying to force the issue was only going to cost him his best friend.

Alexis Ruiz was down the hall, visiting one of the boys from the marching band. Diana was alone in her hotel room, watching a nature documentary in Greek. The language barrier wasn't that big of an issue, given Diana's first supernatural ability; generally, when she watched Animal Planet, she was unable to focus on the narration anyway. What the exotic animals had to say was much more fascinating. Diana was watching a family of Meerkats argue over food when Astin knocked on the door.

Diana turned the TV on mute and got up from the bed. She looked through the peep hole and sighed. Did she have to answer it?

"I know you're in there," Astin said.

Diana unlocked the door and let her brother in. "Hi."

Astin walked past Diana and into the room. He stood by the window, overlooking the busy Athenian street.

"What do you want?" Diana asked. She had been cold to him since August. She had every reason to be since the Titan Atlas had revealed that Astin had murdered her boyfriend with a peanut butter sandwich.

"To talk?"

Diana crossed her arms and just stared at him

"I mean, we used to talk all the time, and now we don't."

"I wonder why that is."

Astin rolled his eyes. "Your anger is noted, Di."

"Yeah, and justified. Is there something important you needed to talk about?"

"I need to fix this."

"Well, you can't."

"I know, but I need to try. Diana, I killed Ryan. I thought he was corrupting you, or hurting you, and then he was coming between us and I just wanted to get rid of him. I just saw him as a threat, someone who was going to break your heart and blow our cover and ruin our lives. But the moment he stopped breathing I realized that I had made a mistake. It was too late. I couldn't take it back. It was a mistake"

"A mistake is something that happens in the moment. You planned it. You actively planned to kill my boyfriend."

"I didn't realize he was *that* allergic. I thought I'd have time to stop it. I thought I could heal him."

"You killed him."

"I know," Astin's voice cracked. "I'm sorry."

"This isn't even your first offense. You did this before. I have memories of you setting me up to kill Orion. You don't even have the guts to do it yourself, you have to trick me into it. It's like you're so threatened that I'll fall in love with someone and stop being your sister."

"I suppose I am."

Diana sat down on the bed and picked up the remote. "Get out," she said.

"I'm sorry," Astin repeated.

"I know. But I'm not ready to forgive you. Get out."

Celene sat in a large arm chair, camped out with her laptop and her step-down power converter in the lobby of the hotel by the elevator. She wasn't going to have a repeat of the night before. She knew that she couldn't reasonably stay up all night until the trip was over, but she thought that staying out until one-thirty would give the impression that she was holding a constant vigil.

Celene restarted her game of solitaire and started clicking through her stack of virtual cards, looking for aces. Bed check was soon. Students would need to be in their rooms, then the real watch began.

The elevator opened and Nick Morrisey stepped out. Celene was ready to jump up and call him a hypocrite for ratting out his friends and then attempting to sneak out on his own, but Nick turned straight for her. He was seeking her out.

"Hey, Dr. D, I was just looking for you."

"Were you?"

"Yep. I wanna show you something." Nick had a newspaper in his hand and he held up the rolled-up issue. "But not here."

Celene looked between her laptop screen and the newspaper. Curfew wasn't for another twenty minutes. She could check-in with Nick, do the sweep, and then come back down here. Surely nobody would sneak out right before bed-check. They would be missed.

"Alright," she said, folding her laptop and unplugging it from the power source. "Let's make it quick."

Celene followed Nick to the elevator.

"So tell me," she said, after pushing the button to return to her floor. "What made you rat them out?" Celene had been turning over Nick's possible motives in her mind all day. He was usually at the root of trouble, right? Of all of the kids in The Pantheon, Celene would peg Nick as the one most likely to sneak out to a nightclub in a foreign country. Why had he stayed behind to tattle?

"We already pushed our luck vanishing through an archway at the Acropolis. I just knew someone like Lewis would do something stupid to get us all exposed. I mean, they almost got caught up in a crime scene, right? Like we need that association added to our record."

Celene wasn't sure she believed it. Was his self-preservation instinct actually stronger than his desire for hedonism? Maybe Jason's speech this summer had worked. The door opened and Celene stepped out onto the plush rug. Nick followed her down the hall.

Celene unlocked her door and looked around. Nobody in the hall. Good. She didn't need to be seen going into a hotel room alone with a student, especially Nick. "Make it quick," she said as he closed the door. "What's in the paper?"

"The guy who was killed was a tourist. American. Nothing special about him. He's from Missouri and he was traveling abroad after college. Some of his friends were at the club with him. They said he had been buying drinks for a girl when they last saw him."

"So the killer is female?"

Nick shrugged, "Or part of a team. Anyway, the police released that all of the victims have been left with a coin in their mouth, as we suspected, but also that their names were carved into the surface they were found on, almost like a burial marker. This guy's was scratched into the toilet."

"Odd," Celene frowned.

"Yeah, so he kills in public places without being seen and then follows Ancient Greek burial rites. Sound like a Titan?"

"Or just a serial killer who happens to be in Athens. What's the timeline?"

"The first associated murder was September. There was a second in October, two in November, six in December, a little cooling off period in January and early February, and then three more in the last two weeks."

"Thirteen."

"But it started right after we killed Atlas."

Celene shook her head. "We can't assume that this is a Titan. All of the Titans thus far have come to us. But, we can't relax either. We've been attacked by three in one year. We can't drop our guard."

"We need to have a meeting when we get home," Nick said. "Olympus, that cave Peter found today, and finding bodies on top of it?"

"And I got a strange email from Jason this afternoon about giving Diana and Frank's baby a haircut."

"A haircut?"

Celene nodded.

"Cryptic."

"It's just not safe to share what's been going on through digital communication. We'll have to meet with everyone in person."

Nick set the newspaper down on the dresser. He sat down on her bed. "That sounds good. Minnie is trying to seize control in Zach's absence, but she's not doing a very good job of being a leader. She and Lewis went off and played Blackjack last night. Real responsible."

Celene raised an eyebrow at him. "You're going to lecture about responsibility?"

Nick stood up, laughing. "Fair enough. But hey, I'm eighteen. Maybe I've just finally decided to grow up."

Celene looked down at her watch. "Bed check is in ten. I can't be seen with you leaving my hotel room. You'd better go." When she looked up, Nick was standing very close.

"You sure you want me to go?" he asked.

Oh hell no, she thought. Celene stepped back. "Nick, get out."

Nick smirked. "You've never been curious?"

"You're a teenager."

"I'm eighteen. It's alright."

"No, it's not. Get out."

"Or do you only sleep with bearded men?"

"It's not funny, Nick. Get--"

The room was plunged into darkness.

"What just happened?" Nick asked.

Celene looked out the window of her room. The lights were still on in every other building on the busy street. "It's just this hotel. A fuse must have blown."

"Well, we could make use of the time--"

"Shut up, Nick. I don't need the lights to put my knee in your crotch. Use the blackout to get out before someone sees you."

"Jesus, fine. Alright." Nick grumbled as he walked to the door.

Celene had expected the backup generator to kick on by now.

"You know where to find me if you change your mind," Nick said.

Celene was just about to answer that she wouldn't when somebody screamed.

"Whatever it is, I fear the Greeks even
when they bring gifts."

-Virgil

xiv.

The great walls had been built by the gods themselves,
and the army of Agamemnon was tired.
No siege weapon was strong enough to breech them.
It fell to deceit.

The wooden horse was presented at the gates.
The fleet of Greek ships receded from the harbor,
and the Trojans took the sign of surrender
as a great godsend.

They brought the parting gift inside the great walls.
After dark the great sculpture began to stir,
and Greek seamen burst with a rallying cry
from inside the horse.

They took torches to every thatched roof about
and slaughtered the surprised Trojans as they slept.
So it came to be that these Greeks bearing gifts
burned the city down.

"Avoid enemies."
-Delphic Maxim

XIV.

"Stay there," Peter said as he made his way to the door of the hotel room. He opened it and peeked out. Other students were looking around the dark hall. The only source of light came from the street lamps, a narrow, dim beam, streaming in through the windows of the open hotel rooms.

The scream repeated. It was coming from below. Another scream joined it.

Diana Hill, alone in her own room, crouched down and put her ear to the floor. When she sat up, her eyes were wide with fear. Someone was being murdered down there. Everyone was running to the emergency exit. It was chaos.

Doors slammed shut as students hid back in their rooms. Peter ducked his head back inside Penny's room for an instant, popped into invisible form, and left the room. "Stay put," he said to Penny before he left. He grabbed her room key off of the dresser so he could get back in.

Peter crept quietly down the hall. Astin was standing outside Diana's room with his hands glowing. Peter stopped next to him.

"Put that shit out," Peter whispered. Astin nearly fell over with surprise, but he extinguished the sunlight from his hands.

"Peter?"

"Screams, Astin. Screams. If someone's on a murderous rampage, don't give them a target."

"I was checking on Diana."

"Great, get in her room and lock the door."

"Where are you going?" Astin asked.

"Call it re-con. The minute I know what's going on, I'm going back to Penny."

"Astin?" Diana whispered through the door.

"Let me in."

Diana cracked the door open and Astin slipped inside.

Diana closed the door. Peter was alone in the hall.

The screams stopped downstairs and everything was quiet. Peter could hear the noise of the busy city outside, but there were no sounds within the hotel. Everyone was frozen in silent terror, waiting to find out what would happen next.

The door to the stairs opened down the hall. Peter pressed himself against the wall. He held his breath as a man stepped into the hall. With all of the doors to the rooms now closed, the hallway was dark. The only light was the glowing red letters of the fire exit sign, running on backup battery. It shone a dim red light on the man, casting his figure as a silhouette. The way he held himself, it was clear that this stranger wasn't a maid or hotel security.

Peter inched down the hall. He held himself flat against Penny's door and waited.

As the man came closer, just a shadow in the dark hall, Peter saw a long knife in his hand. He passed Peter and stopped outside of Diana and Alexis' room to listen. He put his hand on the doorknob and pressed his weight down. The nickel doorknob groaned and snapped. He pushed the door open, but was stopped by the chain. He kicked the door and the chain snapped. The door swung open and the dark hallways was filled with the sounds of broken links scattering about the room. The stranger with the knife stepped inside, but Peter could tell from the cool breeze and the light pouring into the hall that Diana and Astin had already escaped through the window.

Peter looked directly across the hall and saw the door to the opposite room creep open. Evan Fuller peeked out. Evan looked down the hall, setting his eyes on the killer as he stepped into Diana's room. Evan took a deep breath and bolted down the hall towards the emergency exit. Someone in the room behind him slammed the door and frantically locked it. The man with the knife darted out of the room, ready to chase Evan down. It was no good, Evan's crooked run was too slow. What was he thinking? Peter didn't have time to contemplate Evan's stupidity. He took his opportunity and stuck out his invisible foot, tripping the attacker and sending him sprawling across the floor of the hall.

The man didn't even grunt as his body thudded on the carpet. He didn't scramble to get up or roll around in pain. He sat up silently and slowly rose to his feet.

Peter slipped Penny's room key into the lock and ran in. Penny jumped up and slammed the door. She got the chain across the door before the man in the hall started to bang on the door.

"Alright, Penny. Astin's got Diana. Where's Minnie?"

"The guys from Scholar's Bowl invited her to practice Ancient Greek questions in their hotel."

"She's on the boy's floor? Good. The fire-escape."

The doorknob jiggled.

"I need to get to my mom."

Peter ran to the window and looked out. There was an iron fire-escape just outside. "He's coming *now*. You get to the ground level and get help. I'll go get your mom."

The doorknob groaned.

"She's my mom, Peter."

It snapped. The door opened and stopped at the end of the chain.

"I know. I'll make sure she's safe. I'm stealthier alone."

Penny took a deep breath and nodded. "Alright. Keep her safe."

Penny slipped out the fire escape just as the door was kicked open. Peter hid in the corner behind an arm chair and waited until the man with the knife looked around the room and then moved on.

The Blood of Athens

Evan Fuller slammed the door to the stairs behind him and pressed his fingers to the frame. The metal warped and melted, holding the door shut. He just had to hope that his classmates were smart enough to stay in their rooms. If he had been smarter, he thought, he would have stayed. It wasn't his job to stop the killer. Still, he knew what he could do to help; if he had sat in the room and waited, he would have forever blamed himself for whatever happened to his classmates.

Heavy footsteps grew louder in the hall. The doorknob jiggled. Someone slammed into the door. The knob creaked and jolted and then settled, crooked and obviously broken. Someone slammed into the door again and again, and then it was quiet. Evan sighed in relief. The welded doorframe had held up.

Evan turned and ran down the stairs. He knew he had to hurry. There was another set of stairs at the other end of the hall; the killer wasn't completely trapped on the girls' floor.

Evan turned and looked down the stairs. He hated stairs. His limp made him slow-going. Stairs in the dark were really no good. His hand fell on the smooth railing, though, and Evan sat on the edge of it. He had never slid down a bannister before. There was a first time for everything. Evan slid down the first one and stumbled on the landing. The second railing brought him down to the boys' floor. As he approached the door, he tripped on something at-once soft and solid. Evan caught his balance against the door.

He groped around in the dark below him. Whatever he had tripped over was warm and wet and squishy. He realized, as his fingers mapped its features, that it was face with the skin peeled off . There was a dead body slumped before the door.

Evan threw the door open and fell into the hall. A german tourist stood, ready to strike anyone who came through that door with a raised fire-extinguisher. He stopped before he struck Evan, his muscular frame highlighted by the moonlight coming in through the window of his room. "Sind Sie verletzt?" he asked.

"Huh?"

"Are you injured?"

Evan shook his head and held up his blood-stained hands. "Not my blood. There's a body in the stairwell. I need to get to the power. I need to put the lights back on."

Lewis came out into the hall.

"Evan! Where the hell were you? Where's Astin and Peter?"

"I was upstairs. Jess Silver forgot her wallet today and was paying me back for--"

"Doesn't matter. Are the other guys alright?"

"I think Peter tripped the killer for me. The guy went down and there was nobody else in the hall."

The German looked confused.

"Listen," Evan said to Lewis. "I need to fix the power. The screaming started right after the power went out, so unless there's two of them, the killer took out the lights on this floor before he started his spree."

"Yeah, he got the guy refilling the soda machine first," Lewis said. "Then this woman who was getting ice. He turned for me next, but I bolted."

"So any idea where he fried the power?"

A beam of light shone from Nick and Teddy's hotel room. Teddy stood in the doorway, holding up his iPhone to cast light on his allies. "I've got a flashlight app. I'll help you look."

"Do you need my help?" the German tourist asked.

Evan nodded. "Go down the the lobby through the stairs and make sure they're sending help."

"Do you think it's the serial killer?" Lewis asked.

Teddy nodded. "Probably. Did you see his face, Lew?"

Lewis shook his head. "Naw. It was too dark."

As soon as the German went into the stairwell, Lewis took Teddy's phone and dashed around the hall. A few seconds later he shouted, "Down here!"

Evan ran to the light. Lewis was standing next to the soda machine. A door with a Keep Out sign in multiple languages stood open. Two bodies, a man in coveralls and a female tourist, lay in a shared pool of blood in front of the door. They were beyond help. Evan stepped over their bodies, trying not to look at them, and stepped inside. "Hold the light," he said to Lewis. "This should only take a minute."

Celene dialed Penny's room number.

"Uh, hello. The power's out," Nick said.

"Landlines still work when the power is out." She slammed down the receiver. "That proves it's not just a power outage. Someone cut the phones. I'm going out there to get Penny." Their cell phones didn't work in Europe. She would have to go there herself.

Nick stood in front of the door. "No way. You're not opening this door. You heard that downstairs. A generator would have kicked on by now if it were just a coincidence."

"Nick Morrisey, don't you get between a mother and her child. I'm going out there."

Nick shook his head. "I don't feel like dying today, Dr. D."

"Then stay here like a coward. I'm going." Celene grabbed Nick's shoulder and pulled. He moved away from the door, not willing to find out what she would do if she had to be any more forceful.

Celene stepped out into the dark hallway. A tall man, holding a large hunting knife, banged on the door to the stairwell. It was jammed. He turned around and set his eyes on Celene. In the dark, his eyes flashed red.

The shadowy figure began to step towards her. He took his time, making each footfall heavy and solid. Celene looked between the man with the bowie knife and the door to Penny's room. Was it open? Celene couldn't tell from this angle, and she didn't have a key to the room if it was locked. How was she going to pull this off?

The killer continued his approach. A low chuckle growled forth from his throat. "Demeter," he said. Celene's eyes snapped from the door to Penny's room to the killer himself. He was half way down the hall now. "You've come home."

The door behind her opened. "Get in here," Nick hissed from the door. He reached out. He grabbed Celene by the arm. Something struck her front and shoved her back into the room. An invisible force slammed the door shut. "Are you crazy, he's out there!" Peter Hadley said, his head appearing in front of her. "Penny's going down the fire-escape, let's go!"

"He knew my name," Celene muttered.

"Great, he heard someone say it." Nick took her hand and pulled her towards the window.

"No," Celene dug in her heels and stopped. "He called me Demeter."

Peter's body popped into visibility in front of her. "He did what now?"

"He called me Demeter and said 'You've come home.'"

"He's been snapping doorknobs like they're matchsticks," Peter said.

Something banged on the door, then there was a screech like the tip of a steel knife being dragged across metal. Nick stepped out onto the fire-escape. "Good for him. He's a Titan. Even more reason to run. Let's go!"

Evan got the lights back on a few minutes before the police arrived. They had to cut open the door to the stairwell on the fifteenth floor. Nobody could explain how it had been sealed shut. The students of Olympia Heights gathered in the lobby for a headcount as bodies were carted out. There were three dead. The maintenance man and the tourist that Lewis had witnessed being killed, plus the redheaded woman that Evan had tripped over in the hall. They carted her out with a sheet over her face; her remains were so mutilated that the blood soaked through the covering.

There was no sign of the killer. He had vanished into thin air.

Celene's whole body shook as she called off names. Candice Matthews, who had been dragged out of her room by police, sat shaking in a corner, unable to speak. It was up to Celene to call the parents. Thank God nobody from Olympia Heights had been hurt.

"Unless you need medication from your luggage, you're going to have to go home without it," Celene said. "This hotel is an active crime scene. Your luggage will be shipped to you when the police release it. The school's travel agent is arranging for us to go home this morning. The rest of the trip has been called off."

Students groaned.

"Would you rather be dead?" Minnie asked under her breath.

"Point," said Nick.

Lewis had been sure to grab his backpack from the hotel room. He kept it tucked under his chair while the police were around. It contained the shampoo bottles of nectar, which he would split between a few of the girls' purses before they got on the plane.

Peter, who had been pacing at the back of the crowd, sat down on the couch next to Penny.

"Thank you," Penny said, "for getting my mom."

"It was a good thing I did," Peter said. "She was about ready to charge the killer to rescue *you*."

They sat in silence. What else could they say? Three people had died tonight. Besides, what Peter really wanted to tell her, what Peter wanted to tell all of The Pantheon, would have to wait. As soon as they got back stateside, they needed to call a meeting. The Pantheon had to know that they were all in danger, again.

"In War."
-Spartan Epitaph

XV.

As the battle between Zeus and Typhon raged,
the earth beneath their feet trembled and thundered,
and the air crackled with electricity.
Lord Zeus was winning.

But then the monster snatched the sickle Zeus held
and sliced out the sinews from every limb,
leaving Zeus unmoving on the mountain side.
Then he hid the strings.

"As a matter of self-preservation, a man needs good friends or ardent enemies, for the former instruct him and the latter take him to task."

-Diogenes

XV.

It was nearly noon when June awoke. *June Jacobs* was the first thought that ran through her head. She had doodled it on notebooks for years and now it was a reality. Well, it was a reality once she got a chance to take her marriage certificate down to the social security office. Close enough.

She rolled over to look at Zach, the sterile white motel sheets tickling her bare skin as she moved. Zach opened his electric blue eyes and smiled at her. They had spent their week sleeping in and wandering around the old city, a place so beautiful that General Sherman had spared it from burning during the Civil War. The hanging Spanish moss and the horse-drawn carriages set a perfect scene for newlywed bliss.

"It's about time," he said. "I've been trying not to move and wake you."

"We've slept half the day away," she said.

Zach reached across the bed and tucked her hair behind her ear. She scooted closer and settled into his arms. "Your breath smells horrible," she whispered.

"I love you, too."

June played with the short beard that was already growing on his chin. "Maybe you should just let it grow and, you know, trim it."

"I thought you said people didn't trust politicians with beards."

June shrugged, "Well, you've got four years of undergrad before you get to that point."

Zach laughed. "I'm afraid it might grow into an untamable jungle if I let it go."

"You would look good with a beard."

"Then maybe I'll try it." Zach arched his back and stretched. His stomach grumbled. "We need to head back today."

June nodded. "Let's make a deal," she said. "You get up and brush your teeth, then come back to bed for an hour. Afterward we'll get lunch at that adorable tearoom on the square and head home."

"Which square?" Zach asked. "This whole city is a checkerboard of picturesque squares."

"The one with the griffin on the sign."

"Sounds like a deal," Zach said, climbing out of bed. He stopped at the bathroom door. "Wait, did you say an hour?"

June smirked.

"Then you'd better come in here and brush your teeth, too," Zach said with a grin. He ducked into the bathroom and turned the shower on before poking his head out the door. "Actually, you know what? You'd better shower too."

"Zach!"

He walked to the bed and scooped her up, dragging half of the bedding onto the floor.

"What are you doing?"

"Claiming my wife." He carried her into the bathroom and shut the door. They would eventually have to return to the reality of school, responsibility, and secret superpowers. Today was their honeymoon; they could afford to let down their guard, if only for one afternoon.

Zach hadn't been to a gas station since the death of his Thunderbird this summer; the green Roadster that his father had bought him was electric. The only real challenge had been finding a place to plug it in at the hotel.

Still, breaks were needed on the drive from Savannah to Miami to buy drinks and use the restroom. Zach parked at the gas station next to a box truck with an advertisement for bacon on one side, and June headed for the bathroom. He bought a pair of energy drinks and paid at the counter. He walked outside and pulled out his phone to check the time, stopping at the curb to wait for a long white van to park next to his car. At that moment, the screen lit up with a call. It had been on silent all week.

"Doc," Zach said, answering the phone with a smile. "Having a good spring break?"

"Having a terrible spring break," Jason snapped over the phone. "Where the hell have you been? I've been calling you and June for days."

"Woah now," Zach said. "My phone's been silent and June left her's at home. Something happen?"

"The rest of The Pantheon got off a plane in Miami and hour ago."

"Aren't they supposed to be there until Saturday?"

"Things change. There was a serial killer in their hotel. Celene thinks it was a Titan. It knew her name."

Zach rubbed his jaw. He was taking June's advice and growing a beard. He hadn't shaved since the wedding-- which was only a few days ago-- but it looked like two weeks' growth for a normal man. "Which name?"

"The really old one."

Zach set the canned drinks on the roof of his car. "Is everyone okay?"

"Yeah, they're all fine. Evan got the power back on in the hotel. We're having a meeting in two hours, once everyone can get away from their doting parents. Where are you? Are you even in town?"

"I'm forty minutes out. June and I are just coming back from Savannah. We eloped."

"What?!? I'm not touching that with a ten foot pole right now," Jason grumbled. "We've got a Titan looking for us and someone on the mortal side here trying to blackmail me."

"What?"

"You heard me. Get in town and meet at Celene's at nine. I gotta go. Someone's calling."

"Alright. I'll see you soon, Doc."

Zach hung up the phone. June stepped out of the gas station, her red hair fanning out behind her in the wind. She hadn't put it up in its high ponytail for days. She looked genuinely relaxed as she smiled at him. Her smile faltered. "What's wrong?"

"We have a meeting in two hours. Something bad went down in Greece and someone here knows about us."

Zach went around to the driver's side of the car. As he passed by the box truck, June saw someone step out and strike him on the back of the head. Zach went straight down and June screamed. The man who had attacked him just smiled. "Does that help? Screaming? Do people want to get involved?" he asked her.

June tried to focus on his face, but it was ever-shifting. His nose grew and shrank and hooked and flattened. His eyes flashed between blue and black and brown and green. There was no way that he was human.

"Come on, Hera," the attacker said. "I haven't got all night. What is it, two hours until your friends realize you're missing?"

June put her fists up, but she glanced behind her. Could she make it back into the store fast enough? Could she leave Zach, her husband, behind?

He lunged. She swung her fist and struck him across the eye. His head jerked back from the blow. She had never hit anyone like that before, and June was surprised at how much it hurt. Her knuckles throbbed. She hesitated. He lunged forward and grabbed her, pinning her to the side of the green Roadster. With one hand pinching her nose and covering her mouth and his body holding her still, he waited. She struggled to breathe, watching the skin shift around the split skin on his cheek. Her lungs ached and she tried to kick her feet, but he held her down. The edges of her vision darkened and June Herald Jacobs lost consciousness.

"Have a good breakfast men, for tonight we dine in Hades!'"

-King Leonidas

xvi.

Patrocles went into battle wearing the
distinctive armor of the great Achilies.
In doing so he painted a target on
his very own back.

When the body of his cousin was returned,
the hero Achilles was filled with anger
and swore vengeance on Hector, who had slain him.
It was his duty.

But Odysseus, seeing the hero's rage,
went to him and advised Achilles to wait.
So he granted his men a full day of rest
to prepare to fight.

"A good decision is based on knowledge and not on numbers."

-Plato

XVI.

Peter Hadley slid his key into his front door and entered the house. He dragged an old, beat-up, gray piece of rolling luggage behind him. The bag thunked as he dragged it up the carpeted stairs. He set it down in the hall and turned to look into the living room. His father was asleep in the arm chair, drops of beer clinging to his wild beard. Peter set his keys on the table. His father started up.

"What? Why are you home? It's not Saturday."

"We came home early," Peter said.

"I paid for a week."

"You didn't pay for anything, remember?" Peter went into the kitchen and got a glass of water. He leaned on the door frame and watched his father rub his eyes and search the chair for the remote to the TV.

Was he going to ask why they came home early? Didn't the school call him? Peter sipped his water and waited for his father to ask questions. No questions came.

"Why aren't you at work?" Peter asked.

His father's face darkened. "Son-of-a-bitch would rather hire illegals than pay me an honest wage."

"You lost your job?"

"They say we should build a fence. Well the fence won't stop 'em from coming on rafts, will it?"

Peter sat down on the couch. He didn't think that immigration had anything to do with his father's firing. More like inebriation.

"But it's okay. You have a job," his father said.

Peter set down his glass of water. "I'm seventeen."

"And? A job is a job. I was feeding myself when I was your age."

"I have school. I don't work full time."

Peter watched his father's fist tighten and swallowed. Surely he remembered the tape? He wouldn't dare hit Peter now.

"You'll need to sober up and look for another job," Peter said. "I can't pay the rent."

"You ungrateful little asshole."

"I make minimum wage."

"Then ask for a raise."

"You're supposed to be the adult in this house!"

Mr. Hadley took a swing. He was too drunk and missed, hitting the wooden frame on the couch. He cursed and took another swing, but Peter had ducked under his arm. Peter turned invisible, slipping away while his father shouted and stomped around. He made it out the front door and closed it behind him just in time for his phone to ring.

"We're having a meeting," Penny said.

"Alright. Uh... I need a ride."

"Alright. I'll call Astin and Diana to get you on their way. They'll be at your house--"

"No. Not my house. Have Astin come to the gas station."

"Is everything okay?"

"Sure," Peter said. "I just need an energy drink. You know, jet lag."

"Okay. I'll see you in a bit."

"Thanks, Penny."

Jason paced in front of the door at Celene Davis' house. Eleven kids had arrived and were sitting around, whispering about the serial killer in the hotel. Devon held her baby-- now with a buzz-cut-- and tried to keep him quiet. They were all still waiting for Zach and June. They should have been there twenty minutes ago.

Lewis checked traffic reports on his phone. He set it down a bit too hard on the coffee table and shook his head. "Traffic's clear this leg of I-95 and he won't pick up."

"Maybe their car broke down in a dead zone," Evan suggested, breaking away from the group and approaching Jason. "Like, no cell service. Back woods Georgia."

"They weren't that far out," Jason mumbled. He had the sinking feeling that something bad had happened.

"You said he didn't answer his cell all week," Nick suggested from his spot on the couch. "Maybe he's just blowing you off."

"We're not going to accomplish anything just waiting for Zach," Minnie said. "There are thirteen of us here. That's enough to start. We'll fill him and June in when they get here."

Jason sat down in the grey, plaid arm chair. He took a deep breath. Everyone sat down. "We've got a whole handful of problems," Jason said. "Including a Titan in Athens who knows who we are and a blackmailer here in Miami."

"Blackmailer?" Diana asked. "Someone knows?"

"He knows a lot. And he called me when I got off the phone with Zach earlier. He wants to meet tonight."

Celene shook her head. "Meeting with him just confirms that we have something to hide."

"Celene, he says he has photos. I don't think he's bluffing."

"There's a Titan trying to kill us and you want to go out to meet some stranger this late at night?" The sun had already set. Daylight was not on their side.

"Ten, to be exact," Jason said. "And he wants me to bring our leader. That's why I need Zach."

"I'll go," Minnie said. "I mean, in Zach's stead. I know I'm no Zeus, but I am the strategist. I'll have to be good enough."

"I'll go too," Devon said.

"No way," Frank said.

Devon shook her head. "Listen, if someone with ten-ton muscles shows up, the guy will get spooked. Let me go. I can put him in a haze if we need to, throw him off his game."

"Are we sure we need to do this tonight?" Celene asked.

"He's talking about selling it to the press," Jason said. "So yeah. We need to go tonight."

"Then the rest of us stay here," Celene said. "If there's a Titan out there, I don't want you all alone at home."

"Our mom is going to freak. We just got back from Greece," Astin said.

"I'm more worried about your lives than your mom," Jason said. "Come up with an excuse."

Jason stood up and pulled his keys out of his pocket. He had to be at the rendezvous with Spade in twenty minutes. He didn't have time to argue. "Alright. Minnie, Devon, let's go. We're going to be late."

"False words are not only evil in themselves, but they infect the soul with evil."

-Socrates

XVii.

Hippolytus rejected the domain of
the prideful sea-foam goddess, Aphrodite.
As often happens when man rejects the gods,
she got her revenge.

His father had married a handsome woman,
and she, Phaedra, was struck with overwhelming
desire for the man she was to call son.
He rejected her.

Driven to madness by unnatural love,
most poisonous in its unrequited form,
Phaedra charged that the object of her desire
had claimed her by force.

The father, Theseus, was a great hero
who had won three wishes from Lord Poseidon.
Upon hearing these accusations of rape,
he cursed his own son.

Olympia Heights

Lord Dionysus carried out the sentence
and sent a wild bull to torment the son's horse.
Spooked, the horse fled in absolute terror and
dragged the boy to death.

"What it lies in our power to do, it lies in our power not to do."

-Aristotle

XVII.

Jason stepped out of his old Buick. Julius Spade waited just inside the fence to the playground, his un-intimidating frame silhouetted by the buzzing yellow fixture that lit up the jungle gym. Moths flitted around the lamp, casting wide, soft, dancing shadows on the bark mulch spread below the playground equipment. Minnie and Devon ducked down in the car and watched from just over the edge of the window.

"Alright," Jason said. "I'm here. Let's negotiate."

"I'm gonna cut right to the chase, Livingstone. I know one of your kids is Senator Wexler's boy. So I'm not expecting chump change."

"Money," Jason said, with an edge of dark laughter in his voice. "So this all comes down to money. You've got the secret of a lifetime and you're willing to let it go for a little money."

"It's not that little," Spade said. He held out a folded piece of paper. Jason hesitated and took it. "But yeah," he said. "It can all go away."

Jason opened the paper. $25,000. It was a lot for Jason, but not much for such a big scoop. Couldn't he get more from *The National Enquirer* for the story? They paid millions for first photos of celebrity babies, and these were kids with superpowers. Something wasn't right with the number. Maybe Spade didn't think they'd even look at his evidence. Maybe he didn't think he had a story.

"You're serious?" Jason said. "Senator Wexler is worth fifty-six million dollars and you only want twenty-five grand?"

"I don't need much. But you, you need this to go away."

Jason looked back at the paper. It wasn't like Spade could retire on this amount, or even take a year off of work. Jason wondered if this was evidence that he should call his bluff. Maybe the photos weren't that great, or maybe... "This won't be the end of it, will it? You're only asking for twenty-five because you know Teddy can't get this much without going to his father. But you'll be back. You're not going to let it go away, are you?"

"Right now I'd like a new car," Spade said, smiling. "We'll see what my tastes are further down the road. You've got that much, don't you? You've got a saving's account with some life insurance from Mrs. Livingstone. Heck, you can't even buy your daughter a semester at a private college for that."

Jason's fist slammed into Spade's mouth. Spade staggered back, grabbing his lip as blood pooled in his palm. Jason advanced on him again, pushing him and swinging at him. Spade was a private investigator: he'd had his experience with fights. Once he recovered from the shock of realizing that he'd pegged Jason all wrong, he blocked Jason's swing and socked him in the gut.

Minnie saw Jason draw his fist back for the first strike and sprang from the Electra. She blew past the fence and threw her shoulder straight into Spade's side. Her roller-derby check sent him sprawling on the playground bark. Devon wasn't far behind.

"You brought kids?" Spade shouted from his position on the ground. Blood dripped down his chin and spotted his brown coat.

"Yeah," Minnie scowled, "The same kids you're blackmailing. Stay down."

"We're not kids," Devon added. "We're eighteen."

Jason coughed from the blow to the stomach and put his hand on Minnie's shoulder. "Thanks," he said. "I kind of lost it."

Spade spat at Jason, who stepped back and dodged the glob of saliva mixed with blood. "I've got video of your little blonde friend turning that body into sod this summer. I've got photos of the center beating that guy's face in. You don't think I can get someone to pay for it? It might take me a year, but I'll do it. I'll monetize it on YouTube if I have to. Then they'll come for you and your freaks. You'll wish you'd just paid me."

Devon crouched down beside Spade. He stopped talking and stared at her with blank eyes.

"Mr. Spade, right?"

He nodded. "You can call me Julius."

"That's sweet," Devon said. She placed her hand on his cheek. "You know that I'm not a kid, right?"

"You certainly don't look like one."

"No, I don't. And I've just had a baby, so my hormones are really not in balance right now."

Spade nodded. Jason watched hesitantly, wondering if he should interrupt. Was it worth the risk to let Spade go? Would paying him off ever end this?

"Which is why," Devon continued, "You'll have to forgive me." She pressed forward and kissed him. It was brief and Jason could see the disgust on her face as she pulled away. "Go kill yourself."

"Devon!" Jason shouted. "No!"

Devon stood up and spun around. "He's not just threatening me, he's not just threatening you. I have Xander to think of now, so if he insists on blackmail, he leaves me no choice."

"We're not murderers."

"Call it self-defense."

"Devon, there's a better way to do this," Minnie said. "You could order him to destroy the evidence."

"So he can follow us around and find more? My power has a short time-frame: it's not that strong. If it wears off before he can get to the photos, it won't do us any good. This is the only way to be sure."

"I thought you'd learned something this summer," Jason barked.

"About what? About responsibility? I'm a mother now, Doc. I've got to worry about more than just being able to sleep at night. I thought you'd understand."

"Take it back," Jason said. Spade had gotten up and wandered off while they argued, and Jason looked around wildly for him. "Don't do--" Jason's phone rang. "What now?" he growled.

It was an unknown number. Devon planted her hands on her hips and watched Jason. He cursed and slid his finger across the screen to answer his phone.

"Hello?"

The line was quiet for a minute before someone with a voice like nails on a chalkboard spoke. "Is this the mortal speaking?"

"Who is this?"

Jason's question was met with cold laughter. "You know who this is. I'm the reason your masters are holed-up together, shaking in their boots, pet."

"I'm nobody's pet."

"Doesn't matter. You're going to do something for me."

"Why is that?"

"Because I have your friends Zeus and Hera here. They're taking a little nap."

"What do you want?" Jason asked. Minnie's phone vibrated in her pocket. She picked it up and walked away, whispering into it.

"I want to talk. Man-to-Titan. What do you say? Meet me at midnight. Play diplomat."

"Talk? Why don't I believe you? Oh, right, must have been the slasher film you staged at the hotel."

"That was just a little fun. This is business. Meet me on the roof of the high school at midnight. No backup. We'll exchange words." The Titan hung up the phone.

Minnie hung up at the same time. "That was Dr. Davis. She has to go down to the police station to answer some questions. They identified the woman Evan tripped over at the hotel. It was Mrs. Matthews."

"But Mrs. Matthews came back with us on the plane," Devon said.

Minnie shook her head. "No. That was something else."

"That must have been our Titan. He has Zach and June," Jason said. "I have to meet him at midnight. He wants to talk."

"He can't talk over the phone?" Devon asked.

Minnie looked at her watch. "Then we don't have time to chase down Spade. Let's get back to Dr. Davis' house. We need a plan, fast."

Devon and Minnie ran back to the car. Jason lingered for a moment, staring out across the park in the dark. There was no sign of Spade. Minnie leaned across the seats and honked his horn.

"Come on!" she hollered. "Time's not on our side."

"When the tiniest creature defends itself like this against a giant aggressor, what ought we to do?"

-King Agesilaus

xviii.

Zeus had been warned of this battle for ages.
He had sired the hero Herakles for this.
The Gigantomachy was fought to avenge
the fallen Titans.

The Gigantes shook the slope of mount Olympus.
One of them seized the marble column that held
the roof over the palace assembly hall
and cracked the marble.

Herakles was not the only son of Zeus
to fight so boldly in the raging battle.
A blur of gold streaked across the palace floor:
the speedy Hermes.

The Gigante, with his arms around the pillar,
did not see the spritely god enter the room
but he felt the sandals' tread as Hermes ran
straight up the giant's back.

He only stopped his sprint on the giant's shoulders as he raised his golden sword above his head and, plunging its gleaming blade into the flesh, killed the invader.

"The test of any man lies in action."
-Pindar

XVIII.

Peter Hadley watched the Buick Electra pull away from Dr. Davis' house. Most of the Pantheon had gone home to appease their parents and then try to sneak away again. Peter didn't bother. He didn't think his father cared where he was after the fight. For all he knew, Mr. Hadley might have been passed out drunk on the sofa.

Peter sat down on the front step and stared into the dark. He processed everything that had happened, from finding the body in the bathroom, to the chasm that lead to the underworld, to making peace with Penny. And now, once more, he was fearing for his life. When did it ever end? When did they get to be safe? When did Penny get to be safe?

He was pulled out of his thoughts by a familiar feeling, a sensation of cold that sank beneath his skin and into his chest. He spun around to see a spirit standing over his shoulder. It was Mrs. Matthews.

"Oh no. No, no, no," Peter said. "I'm not going to be haunted by you. I've done all of my English homework this semester."

"Jason's in danger," she said, her eyes wide. She placed her hand on his shoulder. Peter felt the icy pressure, even though his shirt didn't so much as crease. "It's a trap. The Titan can change shape. He's going to kill Jason and use his form to get to all of you."

Peter looked down the street. The old Buick was already out of sight.

"Are you sure?"

"He used me to get back here and he'll use Jason to get to each of you, one by one."

Peter swallowed. He nodded. "Alright. Thanks for the warning, but Doc's not in the car. It's Frank."

"Then he'll kill Frank and use him. Nobody is safe. Not you, not Jason, not Penny. You have to act now."

"I will," Peter said. Mrs. Matthew's ghost, a being of cool blue light, glowed brighter until she was a flare of white light. Peter squinted as she grew brighter and then suddenly faded away until Peter was left alone. He looked down at his hands and watched them flicker out of visibility. When he was sure that no part of him was left to be seen, he slipped into the house and grabbed the keys off of the table by the door. Devon was asleep on the couch, baby Xander dozing in his mother's arms. Celene had nodded off in the arm chair. Only Penny was awake.

"Peter?" she whispered.

Peter wanted to say something, but he knew that every word he wanted to say wasn't fair to her, so he pressed his lips together and closed the door. The keys belonged to Frank, and Peter started the motorcycle. He had ridden a cousin's dirt bike years ago, when they still visited the family in Hillsborough county; Frank's bike was heavier and more powerful, but Peter found it almost the same once he got used to it.

He pulled out of the driveway and down the street in the direction of the school. He wasn't sure what he planned to do, but the cold feeling that had settled in when the ghost of Candice Matthews had arrived just wouldn't go away. Though he was sweating beneath his black canvas jacket and Frank's too-big motorcycle helmet, Peter Hadley's heart felt like ice.

Jason turned off the bathroom faucet when he heard the rumble of a motorcycle outside. He peeked through the blinds. Peter, looking like the Mouse on the Motorcycle in comparison to Frank's fierce red Yamaha, was pulling away.

"Son of a--" Jason grumbled. He ran down the hall and out the front door.

A purple jaguar pulled in to Celene's driveway. Teddy didn't even have time to put the car in park before Jason was at the door.

"Hey, Doc, what's up? Was that Peter on Frank's bike?"

"Don't turn off the engine," Jason said. He ran around to the passenger's side door.

"Where are we going?" Teddy asked.

"The school. Peter's about to do something stupid."

With a baseball cap pulled down over his face, Frank Guerrero sat behind the wheel of the Buick Electra, squinting in the dark at the exterior of Olympia Heights Senior High. A light was on in the office at the other end of the building.

Frank turned the collar of his coat up to hide his face, walked to the fence around the air-conditioning units, and checked around once before starting to climb. The climb was easy, but he moved slowly to avoid making too much noise. Frank wanted to catch this asshole by surprise and knock his lights out before he could realize that it wasn't Jason who had pulled-up in the old Electra.

From the fence, to the top of the air conditioner, to the awning, to the conduit, to the roof, Frank climbed. He wondered if the Titan he was meeting could merely fly up to the roof. When he got to the top, he looked down. A pinprick of red light shone at him. Frank smiled and slipped his hand into his pocket. All according to plan.

There was a fixture on the roof, a large box that Frank assumed was the housing for some electrical work. Next to it, in its shadow, stood a man in a long coat. Frank couldn't see his face in the dim moonlight.

"So," he said, raising his voice a bit and doing his best to sound like Jason.

The man stepped out of the shadow and into the moonlight. His face was moving, constantly shifting. It stopped, the features settling on a remarkable facsimile of Candice Matthews' face. His body was still broad and masculine and the result was grotesque. "Looking for someone?" he asked.

Frank grunted. It was best not to speak too much, or he'd give himself away. He kept his head tipped down. Surely the Titan wasn't this stupid, right? Frank was nearly seven feet tall.

The Titan continued in his approach until he was standing right in front of Frank. He smiled and his face began to shift again, slowly this time. "You're not who I expected," the Titan said.

Frank glanced over the Titan's shoulder. Another flicker of a red laser light told him that everything was in position. Frank's eyes focused back on the Titan and he stepped back in shock. The Titan was wearing Frank's own face.

"You're not the mortal," he said, wearing a wicked smile. "You really should learn to follow directions."

Lewis crashed into the Titan's back, tackling him to the ground. They rolled around on the roof, falling into the shadow of a water tank. When Frank grabbed each man by the back of the shirt and pulled them apart, he found himself pinning two identical teenagers to the ground, each held firmly under one large open hand. They were both Lewis Mercer.

"Frank, it's me!" one of them shouted. He grabbed the fingers on Frank's left hand and tried to pull the hand off of his chest.

"Bullshit!" shouted the other. "He's a shapeshifter!"

"Let me go and I'll prove it by super-speeding."

"Don't! We don't even know what the Titan can do. Don't let him go!"

"Come on, Frank, don't you know me well enough by now to know it's me?"

"He's lying. Can't you tell?"

"Alright. Just pummel the hell out of both of us. I'll take one for the team."

"I'm gonna vote to *not* be murdered by fists of rage, here."

"Frank, whatever you do, just do it quick. We have to save Zach."

The Lewis in his left hand seemed to want what was best for The Pantheon. The Lewis Frank knew was eternally loyal to Zach, right? Frank wasn't sure what to do, but he figured that listening to both of them would only make him more confused. He had to trust his gut. Frank took his left hand off of the Lewis it held and struck the Lewis pinned beneath his right hand.

The Lewis he struck went immediately limp and fell to the ground, unconscious but still breathing. The other Lewis, the one he had released, stood up, reached into his pocket, and shot Frank with a taser. Frank went down hard. As he lay panting on the ground, hundreds of thousands of volts still coursing through his body with a benign-sounding click, the face of the Lewis he spared began to shift endlessly.

"Sorry, Ares," he said. His jacket shifted back from Lewis' green track jacket to a long black trench coat. "Wrong choice. Hermes should be flattered that you think he's so selfless." He began to pace around Frank. "I was hoping for the mortal, but you'll have to do."

"A savage desire eats away at you,
drives you to murder, blood-sacrifice pro-
scribed by divine law, whose only fruit is
bitterness."

-Aeschylus

xix.

The four brothers, Prometheus, Menoetius,
Epimetheus, and Atlas, fought on both
sides of the war between the gods and Titans.
The Titans fell back.

With Prometheus on the side of the Gods,
The Olympians were sure to win the war.
Menoetius, a Titan defined by rash acts,
continued forward.

As he reached the palace at Mount Olympus
he was met by the Olympian King, Zeus.
Zeus stared him down with a thunderbolt in hand,
clenched tight in his fist.

From ten meters above him, Zeus hurled his bolt
and split the broad chest of Menoetius in twine.
With his defeat the Titans were all cast down
into Tartarus.

"He is the best man who, when making his plans, fears and reflects on everything that can happen to him, but in the moment of action is bold."

-Heroditus

XIX.

Peter climbed the chain-link fence and scooted up the conduit just in time to see Frank go down. The Titan stood over him, smiling and speaking quietly. Frank twitched on the ground, unable to force his way through the current of electrical impulses and compel his muscles to move. Peter was invisible now, but he still had to be cautious. He walked slowly, trying to minimize the crunch of his boots on the tar rooftop.

A pebble rolled under his foot. The Titan looked up. He sniffed the air.

"I can smell your sweat and fear. Invisible? It must be you, Hades."

Peter revealed himself. He tried to stand tall and proud, but it was hard not to show fear in front of an unknown enemy. "Who are you?" he asked.

"Finally!" the Titan shouted. He put his hand over his heart. "Really, Hades. I'm touched. It's so nice to know that somebody cares." A sick smile spread across his face. "Some call me passion," he sang, "Some call me action, some call me violence, but I prefer *murder*. Menoetius, son of Iapetus." He held out a hand to shake. Peter didn't take it.

"Why Livingstone?" Peter asked. "I mean, you have Zach and June."

"You Olympians don't trust each other, but all of you trust the mortal without a second thought. I'm a god of many talents, but even I can't take on fifteen Olympians at once."

"Why take us on in the first place?" Peter asked.

"Well, there's the whole moral question of dispatching the Olympians for the sake of the mortals, which frankly," he gestured to Frank, unconscious on the ground, the taser still clicking away, "I don't give a damn about that. Then there's the fact that you all murdered my brothers. Prometheus, Epimetheus, and Atlas were much nobler than I am, but they didn't deserve to die. So, yes. I'm going to kill you all for vengeance, and also because I like killing people." The taser stopped clicking. Menoetius dropped it on the ground, letting the plastic shell crack.

"That's why you killed all of those other people?" Peter asked. "Because you like killing?"

"I had to keep myself busy while I waited for you," the Titan said. "And when I get bored, I murder. It's rash, I know, but that's just the way chaos made me." Peter could tell he was excited. He was showing off. Menoetius flicked his hands and his appearance changed in a flash. He was a short man with long hair and an impressive mustache. He

176

spoke in an eastern-european accent. "I've been princes, bloody and terrible." With another flick of his hands, more for show than function, he was another, bearded man holding a scepter and a crown.

Now he was tall with a top-hat and a black Inverness coat. He spoke with a British accent and brandished a knife. "I've inspired theories, movies, and novels."

His form changed again, this time to an Italian man with a red sox hat over his eyes and a thick Boston accent. He twirled a piece of chord in his fingers. "I've inspired copycats, too."

He changed into a man with short hair and heavy glasses, wearing a crosshair on his chest, "And a good handful of frauds."

Now he was back to his shifting form, dressed in a black coat and never letting his face settle too long on one identity. He had walked closer to Peter, and now the young Olympian found himself backed against the ledge.

Peter clapped sarcastically. "I am death, and you are murder," he said, stepping to the side slowly, trying to maneuver himself away from the ledge. "You bring souls for my Kingdom. That would make me your boss, then."

"Nonsense. I'm a Titan. I came before you and I will be here when you are destroyed."

"But if you're murder... that's a very specific kind of death. So you fall under my domain." He had worked his way around so that the line of sight between himself and the Titan was parallel with the edge of the roof. Peter glanced over his shoulder. A purple Jaguar was pulling into the school parking lot.

"It won't be your domain when I kill you," Menoetius said. A long knife grew out of his hand. He wrapped his fingers tight around the handle. "It will be easy," he said. "Especially with our agent among you."

Peter's hands clenched into tight fists. "What?"

"Who do you think released the Titans? Zeus did a fine job of cleaning up after his coup. Even I give you enough credit to know that, had we burst out on our own, you would have had some warning. Someone betrayed you. One of your own."

"Who?"

"Now, Hades, why would I tell you a thing like that?"

"Because you're planning to kill me anyway?" Peter suggested.

"Yes, well, true... but I'm planning to kill Persephone first. I want to keep you alive and make you watch. Maybe I'll have a little extra fun, you know what I mean? Like I taught my little friend BTK. Doesn't that sound like fun?"

Peter blinked out of sight.

"Is that the best you have? You think that your little invisibility trick will keep me from her?" Menoetius asked.

"No," Peter said from behind him. "But this will."

There was a scraping of shoes on tar as Peter charged towards the Titan. Menoetius spun around in time to be struck by an invisible force. Peter's arms wrapped around his shoulders, not giving him the chance to squirm free. The back of Menoetius' calf hit the ledge around the roof.

He clutched at Peter's shirt, his fingers curling around invisible fabric.

From the parking lot Jason watched as a figure in black was knocked back and tipped over the edge of the roof. His black cloak floated out around him as he sailed to the ground and hit the concrete with a thud and a thousand simultaneous cracks.

"Everywhere man blames nature and fate, yet his fate is mostly but the echo of his character and passions, his mistakes and weaknesses."

-Democritus

XX.

It is said that once, a murderer, pursued
by the parents of the man that he had killed,
fled from the city to hide in the forest
and was followed there.

Along the river bed he saw a lion,
and so, to escape the beast, he climbed a tree.
But climbing through the tree he saw a serpent
and so he jumped down.

As he fell towards the surface of the river,
A crocodile popped up and snapped its great jaws.
It caught the murderer and broke his body,
killing him at once.

There is a lesson to be learned from this tale:
when you stoop to take the life of another,
you'll find no refuge on the land, in the air,
nor in the waters.

"A human being is only breath and shadow."

-Sophocles

XX.

"What the--" Teddy jumped out of the driver's seat and chased after Jason as he ran to the fallen man. The Titan lay dead, his face frozen in a distorted mixture of unharmonious features. Jason reached out to check his pulse and felt something invisible block his hand.

"Oh, shit, Peter," he said. He grabbed what he assumed were Peter's shoulders and turned him over. Peter faded back into visibility, his head covered in blood, his limbs twisted and broken.

"Call 911!" Jason shouted, "And then get the hell out of here." He threw his phone at Teddy. Teddy dialed the number, set the phone on the concrete, and ran back to his car.

Frank looked over the edge of the roof. "What happened?" he asked, wiping a thick coating of sweat from his brow.

Jason took off his coat and laid it over Peter to keep him warm. "Don't move Peter," he said, though he wasn't sure if the barely breathing boy could hear him. There was a gurgling response. Peter was choking on blood.

The voice of the 911 dispatcher on speaker phone faded into background noise and Jason worked, trying to help stabilize Peter without any supplies. Frank jumped down off the roof, landing on his feet and sinking into the soft lawn. He had Lewis draped over his shoulder. Lewis was awake, but clearly concussed. "That's Zach's car," Lewis said, pointing to the Tesla Roadster parked hidden in the shadow of the building.

Jason took the keys out of the dead Titan's pocket and threw them to Frank. "Go on," he said as a siren sounded in the distance. "Take it back to Celene's. You can't be found here."

Frank ran with Lewis still over his shoulder.

"Put me down, I'm fine," Lewis said.

Frank ignored him and kept running until he got to the Roadster. He set Lewis down, and Lewis staggered before leaning against the car and holding his head. His face was swelling and turning a deep shade of purple.

"Man, you hit me."

Frank grunted as he unlocked Zach's car and jumped in. Lewis took the passenger's seat.

"You actually thought I was a Titan?"

"Not now. Where the hell are Zach and June?" Frank asked as he started up the car.

"Certainly not in the trunk. That thing barely holds anything... wait." Lewis rubbed his head, "Zach installed a GPS tracker on the car in case it got stolen." He flipped open the glove box. Zach's iPhone fell on the floor. The case looked scuffed, like it had recently been dropped, but it turned on. Lewis logged in to the application for the tracker and held it up show to Frank as they peeled out of the parking lot. "We've got a map of everywhere this puppy has been in the last twenty four hours," he said. "Turn left up here."

The Lightning Green Roadster was out of sight just as the police and ambulance arrived at the school. Sirens wailed and blue and red flashing lights flooded the parking lot, casting Jason's shadow across Peter's still and broken form.

"There is nothing permanent except change."

-Epicurus

xxi.

Lord Zeus called Hephaestus into his chambers
to commission him for a special project.
He had received a visit from his sister
that very morning.

Hestia, the goddess of the hearth and home,
was wearied by the drama of her siblings
and had asked to abdicate her golden throne
on Mount Olympus.

And so Zeus asked the Smith to craft a new throne
for his son, young Dionysus, god of wine.
The fledgling god would take his seat as one of
the Olympians.

"Only the dead have seen the end of war."

-Plato

XXI.

The sleeves of Zach Jacob's suit weren't quite long enough to cover the rope burns on his wrists. He covered the left wrist with the watch his mother had given him for Christmas and covered his right wrist with his left hand. June clung to his arm, her fingers pressing painfully into his bicep as she forced herself not to cry. It was a beautiful, sunny day when they buried Peter.

Across the cheap steel casket, Penny sobbed into her mother's shoulder. The entire Pantheon had shown up, but hardly anyone else had come. Peter's father stood at the head of the casket, stone sober and expressionless. Peter's science teacher and the minister were the only other attendees.

When the service was over, a parade of cars left the cemetery, leaving a lone worker to turn the crank and lower the box into the ground.

Olympia Heights

Zach sat on Celene's couch, still dressed from the funeral. His navy blue trench coat was draped over the back of the couch and his tie was loosened, but he hadn't gone home to change. He sat with his hands folded, his elbows rested on his knees, his fists pressed tight against his mouth. The reality of the last few days was finally settling. Nobody outside the Pantheon could know that Zach and June had been kidnapped or that Lewis and Frank had found them in a storage locker on the edge of town. Peter was dead. They were at war.

"So," started Lewis in an uncharacteristically somber tone, "What now?"

"He told Peter something," Frank said. "I heard it as I was coming to. He said there was a traitor in the Pantheon. Someone who freed the Titans."

Zach's eyes went straight to Nick, who didn't seem to notice the accusing glare.

"Well," June started, "If someone did that, and he wasn't just screwing with us, then they got double-crossed too."

"The Titan, Menoetius: he was the last of the four sons of Iapetus," Minnie said. "Perhaps they're all that's coming."

"Or *perhaps* not," said Nick. "Face it. Peter's dead. The police can't explain who that Titan was or why they were fighting on the roof. They can't explain how everyone saw Mrs. Matthews on the airplane when she was sitting in a morgue in Athens. People are asking a lot of serious questions and nobody has any good answers."

Jason sat in the large arm-chair, silent, his fingers steepled as he listened to the chatter around him. He hadn't spoken since arriving.

"And then there's the blackmailer," Teddy added.

Minnie shook her head, "Spade won't be coming back. They found him dead in his apartment. Well, they found James Harper Junior. Spade was his work alias. There was a little back-page piece in the paper yesterday. Suicide." She looked at Devon when she said this.

"If he's dead," June asked, "Where's the evidence?"

They stared at her.

"You didn't honestly think that his death would erase this, did you? If he says he had photos, someone is going to find them."

"He died without family and the police don't suspect foul play. It'll probably be months before anyone finds the evidence, if they ever do," Minnie said.

"Or maybe he gave them to a lawyer with 'open on the event of my death.' If he saw Frank kill Atlas, he knew he needed insurance."

"I'm still not a hundred percent sure he had evidence," Jason said. "He asked for so little money. He might have been bluffing."

"In a few days when the scene is clear, we need to break in to his apartment and make sure there's nothing to incriminate us," June said. "We can't wait too long or the land lord will clean it out."

"Peter's dead," Penny said.

Everyone stopped and looked at her. Peter hadn't been the most popular guy, but he had grown on them. He might have been dark and distant, but he was one of them. They were a family. You couldn't survive two Titan attacks and a handful of supernatural powers without growing some sort of bond. They all knew that Penny had been close to him. He was Penny's best friend.

"Peter's dead," she repeated after a long, awkward silence, "Peter died to protect us. And that means any one of us is mortal."

"He was going to get away from his father," Jason said. Everyone let that thought sink in. It was no secret that Peter had more black eyes and split lips than were normal. The silence grew thick and heavy as it filled the room, and with each passing second it became harder to speak. What more could be said?

There was a rumbling outside. The engine of a car cut out and a minute later the door creaked open. Valerie Hess poked her head in.

Valerie was their sixteenth member, the goddess Hestia reborn. She hadn't come on the trip and nobody had seen her since lunch at school two Fridays before.

"Valerie," Zach said, "We missed you at the funeral."

"Because nobody told me," she said with tracks of tears running down her face. She closed the door.

Silence.

Valerie shook her head. "Remember, I was in Guatemala with my church. I haven't had phone or internet." She closed her eyes. "Nobody told me anything. I just got home and read about Peter's death on Facebook."

Celene cringed and rose to her feet. She wrapped her arms around Valerie and held her for a minute. Everyone else in the room was out of tears. They shared the misery of stinging eyes and the painful lump that forms in the throat after too much crying. "Come in, Valerie, sit down," Celene said, "I'll make you a cup of tea and we'll fill you in."

"Inferiors revolt in order that they may be equal, and equals that they may be superior. Such is the state of mind which creates revolutions."

-Aristotle

xxii.

The Lord Zeus lay in bed with his wife, Hera.
It was a cool evening in mid-summer.
The gentle breeze was comfortable on his
uncovered shoulders.

The light of the stars cast everything in
indistinct shades of indigo and shadow.
Hera breathed warm against her husband's bare chest.
All Olympus slept.

The darkness came, not as a gradual fade
or the sudden extinguishing of candles,
but as a tidal wave that swallowed the stars:
a blanket of night.

With the darkness came a sudden chill that woke
the King and his Queen from their slumber.
But before Zeus could take up his bolts, it sprang
forth to bind them both.

"He lives not long who battles with the immortals, nor do his children prattle about his knees when he has come back from battle and the dread fray."
 -Homer

XXII.

Jason sat on his sofa, watching Haley and the twins enact a soap opera with mismatched Happy Meal toys. The dialogue blended into white noise as he thought about the last week. Spade had come to him. Menoetius was planning to kill him and take his place. Somehow, as a bystander in all of this, he had become the center of it.

His eyes flicked to the back of Haley's head. She sat, sucked into the drama of their role-play, completely unaware of the trouble that had threatened her world over the last year and a half.

The doorbell rang. "Go play in your room with the twins for a bit, will you?"

Haley pouted.

"I'll bake cookies when I'm done."

The kids bolted to Haley's bedroom and slammed the door. Jason crossed through the mud room and opened the front door. Celene stood alone on the doorstep. She threw her arms around him and buried her face in the crook of his neck.

Jason had found it hard to sleep over the last few days. He felt like something cold and solid had climbed inside his chest and settled there. The weight of it sapped his energy throughout the day and jolted to wake him suddenly every time he drifted towards sleep. He was haunted. Jason thought about all of the ways that he could have done that night differently. How many scenarios could he run through in his head that left Peter Hadley alive? Jason held Celene and felt her warmth spread through him. She even smelled warm, like fresh earth and caramel. When she finally pulled back, Celene stepped into the house and Jason closed the door behind her. He slid his hands into his pockets. Here was a woman he loved, someone he was almost ready to take the plunge with. After the death of his wife, he had finally found someone who made him happy again. But he couldn't do it. He had other responsibilities.

"You wanted to talk to me?" she asked.

Jason looked at the floor. "You know that he was going to kill me and take my place to get to you, right?"

"Well, thank God we sent Frank and Lewis instead."

"Thank God for Peter," Jason said. Frank and Lewis would have been dead without Peter's sacrifice.

They stood quietly for a moment. That was a debt that could never be repaid.

"And you know Spade expected me to raid my kids' college fund to pay him off?"

Celene nodded, "We don't have to worry about that. He's gone."

"And you know I was the one left to burn in your house when Prometheus trapped you all in the jar. I was the one who was supposed to fall off that roof the other night." Jason felt like he owed her a solid explanation for what he was about to do.

Celene took his hand. Jason slipped his hand out of her grasp. "When Felicia died, I thought I would too. But, by some miracle, I'm still here. I have to be. I've got Haley and Jamie and Scotty to worry about. I can't be worrying about the next Titan to pop up, looking for vengeance. I care about you and I care about those kids, but I have to put *my* kids first. What would have happened to them if Menoetius had taken my identity? What would have happened if he had come home to this house while he picked you off, one-by-one. I can't do it. I can't put them at that kind of risk anymore. If it were just me you know I'd be by your side, ready to fight. But it's not just me."

Celene nodded. "I understand. I do."

"I have to cut myself off," Jason said. "I've thought about this a lot and I hate it, but I have to. I can't be involved with any of it."

Celene clasped her hands together. A horrible knot in her stomach told her that this wasn't merely Jason leaving The Pantheon. He was leaving her, too. "This is goodbye, isn't it?"

Jason nodded. There was a lump swelling in his throat that made it hard to talk. He wanted to apologize, to wrap her in his arms and kiss her, but he knew it wasn't the right thing to do. "It is," he said. His voice got stuck in his throat and he had to push to force the next words out. "I'm sorry."

Celene took a deep breath. She nodded. "Alright," she whispered. "Goodbye."

Celene turned and opened the front door. Jason wanted to tell her he loved her, as if that would ensure that she knew how hard this was for him, but he knew that it wasn't fair to leave someone with knowledge like that. "Goodbye," he said.

Celene stepped out into the cool, sunny afternoon. Jason closed the door and leaned against it for a long while. There was no turning back.

June Jacobs hung the last of her clothing in Zach's closet. His half of the closet was a random assortment of jerseys, dress shirts, pants hangers, and jackets. June's half was organized by type (sweaters, tank tops, blouses, skirts) and then color (rainbow order). Obsessive organization was how June handled her feelings. It was much easier to sort articles of clothing than to think about her father shouting that she had thrown her life away by marrying Zach Jacobs in high school.

Zach returned to the house from his trip to the mailbox and threw a pile of bills on the counter for his mother. Beneath his issue of *Sports Illustrated* was a postcard addressed to him. He hadn't gotten a chance to check it out or read it. He was too enthralled in the latest article about upcoming college football prospects (he was still choosing between scholarship offers at Florida State and Auburn) to pay much attention to it.

Zach wandered back to the bedroom and threw a wedding card, the post card, and his car insurance bill on the bed while he read the article. June grabbed for the wedding card, hoping it held money, when she spotted the postcard. It was from the Canary Islands and featured a picture of a mountain, Mount Tiede, against a clear blue sky.

"Zach," she said, her tone urgent.

"What?" he asked, turning the page of his magazine.

"Zach," she snapped, "Look!"

Zach sighed, but smiled, and put down the magazine. He took the postcard. When his eyes settled on the message, the smile vanished from his lips.

I'll be seeing you soon.

~Kronos

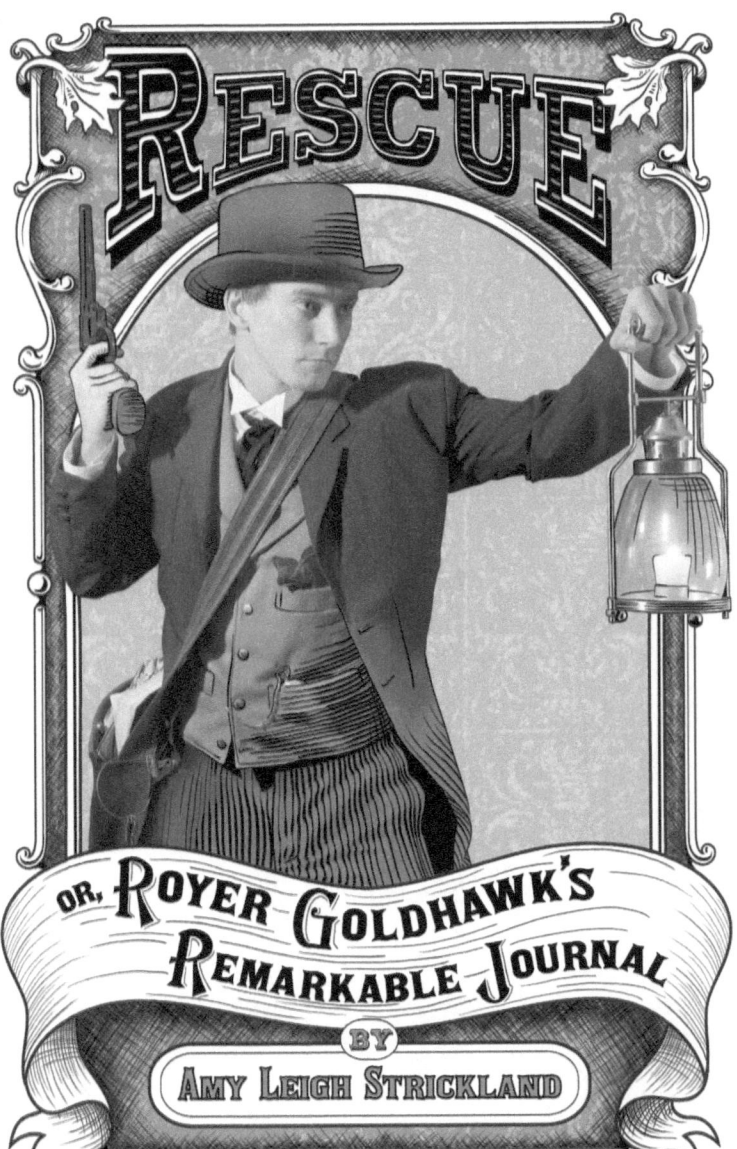

RESCUE

or, ROYER GOLDHAWK'S REMARKABLE JOURNAL

BY

AMY LEIGH STRICKLAND

And now for a preview of the first book in Amy Leigh Strickland's new series:

Rescue OR, Royer Goldhawk's Remarkable Journey

Available May 2013

———◆———

"It is too thick to pass here," Benjy said. I marveled at the thousands of people marching, wondering how many were risking their jobs to be there. Benjy pointed back towards the theater. "Let's go wait for America with Mercy," he suggested. I was up for any excuse to spend more time near Miss Winmer and nodded my head.

Benjy and I entered the alley next to the theater. Up ahead, Mercy waited at the back door, fighting to keep her extravagant hat from blowing off in the breeze that swept through the alley. Benjy called out and she turned to wave. A great shadow fell over the alley and I became acutely aware of a rumble overhead.

I placed my hand on the rim of my hat to keep it from falling off as I looked up at the sky. Overhead, a great dirigible loomed. The rigid airship was being steered directly over the alley and had slowed to linger above us. "Brooker & Bedloe Steam Industries" was painted on the side in a text style that resembled a circus poster. I marveled at the great airship, wondering if it was a part of the parade. Surely a great company like Brooker & Bedloe did not want to encourage their workers to organize, but there was no other explanation for the great ship to fly so low over the city.

As I watched, something seemed to drop from the back of the gondola. It landed in the alley before I could identify it and exploded in a cloud of grey smoke. I fell back, my body automatically throwing me away from the source of danger.

There was a zipping noise, metal quickly grinding against steel cable. A cluster of figures appeared in the smoke, and I could see bodies moving through the cloud in the direction of Mercy Winmer. Her scream was cut off by a fit of choking coughs. One of the figures in the smoke turned and looked at me, and I could see that his face was covered by a long, black mask with great glass eyes. I had seen drawings of similar apparatuses in the journals my father subscribed to; it was a gas mask.

I sprang to my feet as fast as I could and ran back into the cloud, untucking my ascot from the front of my vest and holding it over my nose to filter some of the smoke. A ladder had dropped down from the dirigible and one of the men was pulling Mercy Winmer, now unconscious, towards it. I grabbed for her, but a third figure stepped out of the thick smoke and struck me with something hard. The object hit me just above my eyebrow and the sharp blow stunned me.

The ladder began to rise up evenly, as if pulled by a mechanical crank. It was out of reach by the time I recovered from the blow, so I grabbed the ladder to the fire-escape and began to climb frantically. I could hear Benjy behind me, calling my name, but his voice had receded to the background. Quickly, I scaled the fire-escape and made my way to the top of the roof. I rose above the cloud of slowly dissipating smoke. From the roof of the theater, I was almost level with the gondola. The door was open and someone was reaching out to help the kidnappers haul Miss Winmer inside.

The man in charge-- I assume this because he was dressed in a finely embroidered tailcoat that indicated that he likely had too much money to answer to anyone-- took Mercy Winmer by the arm. He was a handsome older man with thick, pepper-gray hair and a small, neatly-kept mustache. He wore a white silk opera scarf and a red fez. A machine-rolled cigarette hung out of the corner of his mouth, its smoke mixing with the fog rising up from the alley below. He looked at me, his cold, black eyes locking with my own blue ones, and I was stricken by a sense of familiarity. I had met this man before. He smiled and turned back to his business, as if I was a mere observer and clearly no threat to his plot.

I ran. I ran straight up to the edge of the roof and jumped, reaching for the ladder. They would have to knock me off or kill me to stop me. My jump fell short and I grasped desperately, trying to grab something to hold on to. The rich man had a leather tube hanging from a strap around his shoulder, and I managed to grab it. I fell and held on tight. He desperately grabbed the ladder so that I would not pull him down with me. I hung there for a moment, an almost immeasurable instant, before the leather strap stretched and snapped.

Still gripping the tube, I plummeted towards the ground. My fall was broken by the awning over the theater door. It, too, broke and in seconds I was on the ground. I strained to breathe. My side burned. A striped piece of canvas covered my face. It was a moment before I could think to move, to free myself from the broken awning. When I uncovered my own face, Benjy was standing over me in a thin fog and the airship was rising up into the sky. They had gotten away.

Sign up here to receive email notifications about the Royer Goldhawk series:

http://matterdeeppublishing.us2.list-manage.com/subscribe
?u=b4df4845a9856314342a28633&id=3ecae51a7f

Or here for the Olympia Heights series:

http://www.olympia-heights.com/coming-soon/

matterdeeppublishing.com/

About the Author

Amy Leigh Strickland is a writer and teacher from Townsend, Massachusetts. She has a BFA from the Savannah College *of* Art *and* Design and is currently working towards her Masters of Education at the University *of* Montevallo. Amy currently lives outside Birmingham, Alabama with her husband, Kyle and their terrier, Apollo.

Amy blogs about reading, writing, and roller derby at amyleighstrickland.com.

This book was set in 10.75 point Sabon. All
interior decorative type was set in Diogenes, an
open source typeface, by Apostrophic Labs, which
can be found at dafont.com.
Cover Design and Typeset by Carly Strickland
(carlystricklandart.com)